J.R.R. TOLKIEN

THE LORD OF THE RINGS
comprising:

BOOK ONE
THE RING SETS OUT

BOOK TWO
THE RING GOES SOUTH

BOOK THREE
THE TREASON OF ISENGARD

BOOK FOUR
THE RING GOES EAST

BOOK FIVE
THE WAR OF THE RING

BOOK SIX
THE END OF THE THIRD AGE

and

APPENDICES

THE END OF
THE THIRD AGE

BEING THE SIXTH BOOK OF
THE LORD OF THE RINGS

BY

J.R.R. TOLKIEN

HarperCollins*Publishers*

HarperCollins*Publishers*
77–85 Fulham Palace Road,
Hammersmith, London W6 8JB
www.**fire**and**water**.com

Seven-volume edition 1999
1 3 5 7 9 8 6 4 2

First published in Great Britain by
George Allen & Unwin 1955
Second edition 1966
This new reset edition published
by HarperCollins*Publishers* 1994

 ® is a registered trademark of
The J.R.R. Tolkien Estate Limited

ISBN 0 261 10398 9

Set in Postscript Monotype Plantin Light by
Rowland Phototypesetting Ltd,
Bury St Edmunds, Suffolk

Printed and bound in Great Britain by
Clays Ltd, St Ives plc

CONTENTS

I	The Tower of Cirith Ungol	5
II	The Land of Shadow	30
III	Mount Doom	52
IV	The Field of Cormallen	73
V	The Steward and the King	87
VI	Many Partings	107
VII	Homeward Bound	127
VIII	The Scouring of the Shire	138
IX	The Grey Havens	169

Three Rings for the Elven-kings under the sky,
Seven for the Dwarf-lords in their halls of stone,
Nine for Mortal Men doomed to die,
One for the Dark Lord on his dark throne
In the Land of Mordor where the Shadows lie.
One Ring to rule them all, One Ring to find them,
One Ring to bring them all and in the darkness bind them
In the Land of Mordor where the Shadows lie.

CHAPTER I

THE TOWER OF CIRITH UNGOL

Sam roused himself painfully from the ground. For a moment he wondered where he was, and then all the misery and despair returned to him. He was in the deep dark outside the under-gate of the orcs' stronghold; its brazen doors were shut. He must have fallen stunned when he hurled himself against them; but how long he had lain there he did not know. Then he had been on fire, desperate and furious; now he was shivering and cold. He crept to the doors and pressed his ears against them.

Far within he could hear faintly the voices of orcs clamouring, but soon they stopped or passed out of hearing, and all was still. His head ached and his eyes saw phantom lights in the darkness, but he struggled to steady himself and think. It was clear at any rate that he had no hope of getting into the orc-hold by that gate; he might wait there for days before it was opened, and he could not wait: time was desperately precious. He no longer had any doubt about his duty: he must rescue his master or perish in the attempt.

'The perishing is more likely, and will be a lot easier anyway,' he said grimly to himself, as he sheathed Sting and turned from the brazen doors. Slowly he groped his way back in the dark along the tunnel, not daring to use the elven-light; and as he went he tried to fit together the events since Frodo and he had left the Cross-roads. He wondered what the time was. Somewhere between one day and the next, he supposed; but even of the days he had quite lost count. He was in a land of darkness where the days of the world seemed forgotten, and where all who entered were forgotten too.

'I wonder if they think of us at all,' he said, 'and what is happening to them all away there.' He waved his hand vaguely in the air before him; but he was in fact now facing southwards, as he came back to Shelob's tunnel, not west. Out westward in the world it was drawing to noon upon the fourteenth day of March in the Shire-reckoning, and even now Aragorn was leading the black fleet from Pelargir, and Merry was riding with the Rohirrim down the Stonewain Valley, while in Minas Tirith flames were rising and Pippin watched the madness growing in the eyes of Denethor. Yet amid all their cares and fear the thoughts of their friends turned constantly to Frodo and Sam. They were not forgotten. But they were far beyond aid, and no thought could yet bring any help to Samwise Hamfast's son; he was utterly alone.

He came back at last to the stone door of the orc-passage, and still unable to discover the catch or bolt that held it, he scrambled over as before and dropped softly to the ground. Then he made his way stealthily to the outlet of Shelob's tunnel, where the rags of her great web were still blowing and swaying in the cold airs. For cold they seemed to Sam after the noisome darkness behind; but the breath of them revived him. He crept cautiously out.

All was ominously quiet. The light was no more than that of dusk at a dark day's end. The vast vapours that arose in Mordor and went streaming westward passed low overhead, a great welter of cloud and smoke now lit again beneath with a sullen glow of red.

Sam looked up towards the orc-tower, and suddenly from its narrow windows lights stared out like small red eyes. He wondered if they were some signal. His fear of the orcs, forgotten for a while in his wrath and desperation, now returned. As far as he could see, there was only one possible course for him to take: he must go on and try to find the main entrance to the dreadful tower; but his knees felt weak, and he found that he was trembling. Drawing his eyes down from the tower and the horns of the Cleft before him, he forced his unwilling feet to obey him, and slowly, listening with all his ears, peering into the dense shadows of the rocks beside the way, he retraced his steps, past the place where Frodo fell, and still the stench of Shelob lingered, and then on and up, until he stood again in the very cleft where he had put on the Ring and seen Shagrat's company go by.

There he halted and sat down. For the moment he could drive himself no further. He felt that if once he went beyond the crown of the pass and took one step veritably down into the land of Mordor, that step would be irrevocable. He could never come back. Without any clear purpose he drew out the Ring and put it on again. Immediately he felt the great burden of its weight, and felt afresh, but now more strong and urgent than ever, the malice of the Eye of Mordor, searching, trying to pierce the shadows that it had made for its own defence, but which now hindered it in its unquiet and doubt.

As before, Sam found that his hearing was sharpened, but that to his sight the things of this world seemed thin and vague. The rocky walls of the path were pale, as if seen through a mist, but still at a distance he heard the bubbling of Shelob in her misery; and harsh and clear, and very close it seemed, he heard cries and the clash of metal. He sprang to his feet, and pressed himself against the wall beside the road. He was glad of the Ring, for here was yet another company of orcs on the march. Or so at first he thought. Then suddenly he realized that it was not so, his hearing had deceived him: the orc-cries came from the tower, whose topmost horn was now right above him, on the left hand of the Cleft.

Sam shuddered and tried to force himself to move. There was plainly some devilry going on. Perhaps in spite of all orders the cruelty of the orcs had mastered them, and they were tormenting Frodo, or even savagely hacking him to pieces. He listened; and as he did a gleam of hope came to him. There could not be much doubt: there was fighting in the tower, the orcs must be at war among themselves, Shagrat and Gorbag had come to blows. Faint as was the hope that his guess brought him, it was enough to rouse him. There might be just a chance. His love for Frodo rose above all other thoughts, and forgetting his peril he cried aloud: 'I'm coming, Mr. Frodo!'

He ran forward to the climbing path, and over it. At once the road turned left and plunged steeply down. Sam had crossed into Mordor.

He took off the Ring, moved it may be by some deep premonition of danger, though to himself he thought only that he wished to see more clearly. 'Better have a look at the worst,' he muttered. 'No good blundering about in a fog!'

Hard and cruel and bitter was the land that met his gaze. Before his feet the highest ridge of the Ephel Dúath fell steeply in great cliffs down into a dark trough, on the further side of which there rose another ridge, much lower, its edge notched and jagged with crags like fangs that stood out black against the red light behind them: it was the grim Morgai, the inner ring of the fences of the land. Far beyond it, but almost straight ahead, across a wide lake of darkness dotted with tiny fires, there was a great burning glow; and from it rose in huge columns a swirling smoke, dusty red at the roots, black above where it merged into the billowing canopy that roofed in all the accursed land.

Sam was looking at Orodruin, the Mountain of Fire. Ever and anon the furnaces far below its ashen cone would grow hot and with a great surging and throbbing pour forth rivers of molten rock from chasms in its sides. Some would flow blazing towards Barad-dûr down great channels; some would wind their way into the stony plain, until they cooled and lay like twisted dragon-shapes vomited from the tormented earth. In such an hour of labour Sam beheld Mount Doom, and the light of it, cut off by the high screen of the Ephel Dúath from those who climbed up the path from the West, now glared against the stark rock faces, so that they seemed to be drenched with blood.

In that dreadful light Sam stood aghast, for now, looking

to his left, he could see the Tower of Cirith Ungol in all its strength. The horn that he had seen from the other side was only its topmost turret. Its eastern face stood up in three great tiers from a shelf in the mountain-wall far below; its back was to a great cliff behind, from which it jutted out in pointed bastions, one above the other, diminishing as they rose, with sheer sides of cunning masonry that looked north-east and south-east. About the lowest tier, two hundred feet below where Sam now stood, there was a battlemented wall enclosing a narrow court. Its gate, upon the near south-eastern side, opened on a broad road, the outer parapet of which ran upon the brink of a precipice, until it turned south-ward and went winding down into the darkness to join the road that came over the Morgul Pass. Then on it went through a jagged rift in the Morgai out into the valley of Gorgoroth and away to Barad-dûr. The narrow upper way on which Sam stood leapt swiftly down by stair and steep path to meet the main road under the frowning walls close to the Tower-gate.

As he gazed at it suddenly Sam understood, almost with a shock, that this stronghold had been built not to keep enemies out of Mordor, but to keep them in. It was indeed one of the works of Gondor long ago, an eastern outpost of the defences of Ithilien, made when, after the Last Alliance, Men of Westernesse kept watch on the evil land of Sauron where his creatures still lurked. But as with Narchost and Carchost, the Towers of the Teeth, so here too the vigilance had failed, and treachery had yielded up the Tower to the Lord of the Ringwraiths, and now for long years it had been held by evil things. Since his return to Mordor, Sauron had found it useful; for he had few servants but many slaves of fear, and still its chief purpose as of old was to prevent escape from Mordor. Though if an enemy were so rash as to try to enter that land secretly, then it was also a last unsleeping guard against any that might pass the vigilance of Morgul and of Shelob.

Only too clearly Sam saw how hopeless it would be for

him to creep down under those many-eyed walls and pass the watchful gate. And even if he did so, he could not go far on the guarded road beyond: not even the black shadows, lying deep where the red glow could not reach, would shield him long from the night-eyed orcs. But desperate as that road might be, his task was now far worse: not to avoid the gate and escape, but to enter it, alone.

His thought turned to the Ring, but there was no comfort there, only dread and danger. No sooner had he come in sight of Mount Doom, burning far away, than he was aware of a change in his burden. As it drew near the great furnaces where, in the deeps of time, it had been shaped and forged, the Ring's power grew, and it became more fell, untameable save by some mighty will. As Sam stood there, even though the Ring was not on him but hanging by its chain about his neck, he felt himself enlarged, as if he were robed in a huge distorted shadow of himself, a vast and ominous threat halted upon the walls of Mordor. He felt that he had from now on only two choices: to forbear the Ring, though it would tor-ment him; or to claim it, and challenge the Power that sat in its dark hold beyond the valley of shadows. Already the Ring tempted him, gnawing at his will and reason. Wild fantasies arose in his mind; and he saw Samwise the Strong, Hero of the Age, striding with a flaming sword across the darkened land, and armies flocking to his call as he marched to the overthrow of Barad-dûr. And then all the clouds rolled away, and the white sun shone, and at his command the vale of Gorgoroth became a garden of flowers and trees and brought forth fruit. He had only to put on the Ring and claim it for his own, and all this could be.

In that hour of trial it was the love of his master that helped most to hold him firm; but also deep down in him lived still unconquered his plain hobbit-sense: he knew in the core of his heart that he was not large enough to bear such a burden, even if such visions were not a mere cheat to betray him. The one small garden of a free gardener was all his need and due, not a garden swollen to a realm; his own hands to use, not the hands of others to command.

'And anyway all these notions are only a trick,' he said to himself. 'He'd spot me and cow me, before I could so much as shout out. He'd spot me, pretty quick, if I put the Ring on now, in Mordor. Well, all I can say is: things look as hopeless as a frost in spring. Just when being invisible would be really useful, I can't use the Ring! And if ever I get any further, it's going to be nothing but a drag and a burden every step. So what's to be done?'

He was not really in any doubt. He knew that he must go down to the gate and not linger any more. With a shrug of his shoulders, as if to shake off the shadow and dismiss the phantoms, he began slowly to descend. With each step he seemed to diminish. He had not gone far before he had shrunk again to a very small and frightened hobbit. He was now passing under the very walls of the Tower, and the cries and sounds of fighting could be heard with his unaided ears. At the moment the noise seemed to be coming from the court behind the outer wall.

Sam was about half way down the path when out of the dark gateway into the red glow there came two orcs running. They did not turn towards him. They were making for the main road; but even as they ran they stumbled and fell to the ground and lay still. Sam had seen no arrows, but he guessed that the orcs had been shot down by others on the battlements or hidden in the shadow of the gate. He went on, hugging the wall on his left. One look upward had shown him that there was no hope of climbing it. The stone-work rose thirty feet, without a crack or ledge, to overhanging courses like inverted steps. The gate was the only way.

He crept on; and as he went he wondered how many orcs lived in the Tower with Shagrat, and how many Gorbag had, and what they were quarrelling about, if that was what was happening. Shagrat's company had seemed to be about forty, and Gorbag's more than twice as large; but of course Shagrat's patrol had only been a part of his garrison. Almost certainly they were quarrelling about Frodo, and the spoil. For a second Sam halted, for suddenly things seemed clear to him, almost as if he had seen them with his eyes. The mithril coat! Of course, Frodo was wearing it, and they would find it. And from what Sam had heard Gorbag would covet it. But the orders of the Dark Tower were at present Frodo's only protection, and if they were set aside, Frodo might be killed out of hand at any moment.

'Come on, you miserable sluggard!' Sam cried to himself. 'Now for it!' He drew Sting and ran towards the open gate. But just as he was about to pass under its great arch he felt a shock: as if he had run into some web like Shelob's, only invisible. He could see no obstacle, but something too strong for his will to overcome barred the way. He looked about, and then within the shadow of the gate he saw the Two Watchers.

They were like great figures seated upon thrones. Each had three joined bodies, and three heads facing outward, and inward, and across the gateway. The heads had vulture-faces, and on their great knees were laid clawlike hands. They seemed to be carved out of huge blocks of stone, immovable, and yet they were aware: some dreadful spirit of evil vigilance abode in them. They knew an enemy. Visible or invisible none could pass unheeded. They would forbid his entry, or his escape.

Hardening his will Sam thrust forward once again, and halted with a jerk, staggering as if from a blow upon his breast and head. Then greatly daring, because he could think of nothing else to do, answering a sudden thought that came to him, he drew slowly out the phial of Galadriel and held it up. Its white light quickened swiftly, and the shadows under the dark arch fled. The monstrous Watchers sat there cold and still, revealed in all their hideous shape. For a moment Sam caught a glitter in the black stones of their eyes, the very malice of which made him quail; but slowly he felt their will waver and crumble into fear.

He sprang past them; but even as he did so, thrusting the phial back into his bosom, he was aware, as plainly as if a bar of steel had snapped to behind him, that their vigilance was renewed. And from those evil heads there came a high shrill cry that echoed in the towering walls before him. Far up above, like an answering signal, a harsh bell clanged a single stroke.

'That's done it!' said Sam. 'Now I've rung the front-door bell! Well, come on somebody!' he cried. 'Tell Captain Shagrat that the great Elf-warrior has called, with his elf-sword too!'

There was no answer. Sam strode forward. Sting glittered blue in his hand. The courtyard lay in deep shadow, but he could see that the pavement was strewn with bodies. Right at his feet were two orc-archers with knives sticking in their backs. Beyond lay many more shapes; some singly as they had been hewn down or shot; others in pairs, still grappling one another, dead in the very throes of stabbing, throttling, biting. The stones were slippery with dark blood.

Two liveries Sam noticed, one marked by the Red Eye, the other by a Moon disfigured with a ghastly face of death; but he did not stop to look more closely. Across the court a great door at the foot of the Tower stood half open, and a red light came through; a large orc lay dead upon the threshold. Sam sprang over the body and went in; and then he peered about at a loss.

A wide and echoing passage led back from the door towards the mountain-side. It was dimly lit with torches flaring in brackets on the walls but its distant end was lost in gloom. Many doors and openings could be seen on this side and that; but it was empty save for two or three more bodies sprawling on the floor. From what he had heard of the captains' talk Sam knew that, dead or alive, Frodo would most likely be found in a chamber high up in the turret far above; but he might search for a day before he found the way.

'It'll be near the back, I guess,' Sam muttered. 'The whole

Tower climbs backwards-like. And anyway I'd better follow these lights.'

He advanced down the passage, but slowly now, each step more reluctant. Terror was beginning to grip him again. There was no sound save the rap of his feet, which seemed to grow to an echoing noise, like the slapping of great hands upon the stones. The dead bodies; the emptiness; the dank black walls that in the torchlight seemed to drip with blood; the fear of sudden death lurking in doorway or shadow; and behind all his mind the waiting watchful malice at the gate: it was almost more than he could screw himself to face. He would have welcomed a fight – with not too many enemies at a time – rather than this hideous brooding uncertainty. He forced himself to think of Frodo, lying bound or in pain or dead somewhere in this dreadful place. He went on.

He had passed beyond the torchlight, almost to a great arched door at the end of the passage, the inner side of the under-gate, as he rightly guessed, when there came from high above a dreadful choking shriek. He stopped short. Then he heard feet coming. Someone was running in great haste down an echoing stairway overhead.

His will was too weak and slow to restrain his hand. It dragged at the chain and clutched the Ring. But Sam did not put it on; for even as he clasped it to his breast, an orc came clattering down. Leaping out of a dark opening at the right, it ran towards him. It was no more than six paces from him when, lifting its head, it saw him; and Sam could hear its gasping breath and see the glare in its bloodshot eyes. It stopped short aghast. For what it saw was not a small fright-ened hobbit trying to hold a steady sword: it saw a great silent shape, cloaked in a grey shadow, looming against the wavering light behind; in one hand it held a sword, the very light of which was a bitter pain, the other was clutched at its breast, but held concealed some nameless menace of power and doom.

For a moment the orc crouched, and then with a hideous yelp of fear it turned and fled back as it had come. Never was any dog more heartened when its enemy turned tail than Sam at this unexpected flight. With a shout he gave chase.

'Yes! The Elf-warrior is loose!' he cried. 'I'm coming. Just you show me the way up, or I'll skin you!'

But the orc was in its own haunts, nimble and well-fed. Sam was a stranger, hungry and weary. The stairs were high and steep and winding. Sam's breath began to come in gasps. The orc had soon passed out of sight, and now only faintly could be heard the slapping of its feet as it went on and up. Every now and again it gave a yell, and the echo ran along the walls. But slowly all sound of it died away.

Sam plodded on. He felt that he was on the right road, and his spirits had risen a good deal. He thrust the Ring away and tightened his belt. 'Well, well!' he said. 'If only they all take such a dislike to me and my Sting, this may turn out better than I hoped. And anyway it looks as if Shagrat, Gorbag, and company have done nearly all my job for me. Except for that little frightened rat, I do believe there's nobody left alive in the place!'

And with that he stopped, brought up hard, as if he had hit his head against the stone wall. The full meaning of what he had said struck him like a blow. Nobody left alive! Whose had been that horrible dying shriek? 'Frodo, Frodo! Master!' he cried half sobbing. 'If they've killed you, what shall I do? Well, I'm coming at last, right to the top, to see what I must.'

Up, up he went. It was dark save for an occasional torch flaring at a turn, or beside some opening that led into the higher levels of the Tower. Sam tried to count the steps, but after two hundred he lost his reckoning. He was moving quietly now; for he thought that he could hear the sound of voices talking, still some way above. More than one rat remained alive it seemed.

All at once, when he felt that he could pump out no more breath, nor force his knees to bend again, the stair ended. He stood still. The voices were now loud and near. Sam peered about. He had climbed right to the flat roof of the third and highest tier of the Tower: an open space, about twenty yards across, with a low parapet. There the stair was covered by a small domed chamber in the midst of the roof, with low doors facing east and west. Eastward Sam could see the plain of Mordor vast and dark below, and the burning mountain far away. A fresh turmoil was surging in its deep wells, and the rivers of fire blazed so fiercely that even at this distance of many miles the light of them lit the tower-top with a red glare. Westward the view was blocked by the base of the great turret that stood at the back of this upper court and reared its horn high above the crest of the encircling hills. Light gleamed in a window-slit. Its door was not ten yards from where Sam stood. It was open but dark, and from just within its shadow the voices came.

At first Sam did not listen; he took a pace out of the eastward door and looked about. At once he saw that up here the fighting had been fiercest. All the court was choked with dead orcs, or their severed and scattered heads and limbs. The place stank of death. A snarl followed by a blow and a cry sent him darting back into hiding. An orc-voice rose in anger, and he knew it again at once, harsh, brutal, cold. It was Shagrat speaking, Captain of the Tower.

'You won't go again, you say? Curse you, Snaga, you little maggot! If you think I'm so damaged that it's safe to flout me, you're mistaken. Come here, and I'll squeeze your eyes out, like I did to Radbug just now. And when some new lads come, I'll deal with you: I'll send you to Shelob.'

'They won't come, not before you're dead anyway,' answered Snaga surlily. 'I've told you twice that Gorbag's swine got to the gate first, and none of ours got out. Lagduf and Muzgash ran through, but they were shot. I saw it from a window, I tell you. And they were the last.'

'Then you must go. I must stay here anyway. But I'm hurt. The Black Pits take that filthy rebel Gorbag!' Shagrat's voice trailed off into a string of foul names and curses. 'I gave him better than I got, but he knifed me, the dung, before I throttled him. You must go, or I'll eat you. News must get through to Lugbúrz, or we'll both be for the Black Pits. Yes, you too. You won't escape by skulking here.'

'I'm not going down those stairs again,' growled Snaga, 'be you captain or no. Nar! Keep your hands off your knife, or I'll put an arrow in your guts. You won't be a captain long when They hear about all these goings-on. I've fought for the Tower against those stinking Morgul-rats, but a nice mess you two precious captains have made of things, fighting over the swag.'

'That's enough from you,' snarled Shagrat. 'I had my orders. It was Gorbag started it, trying to pinch that pretty shirt.'

'Well, you put his back up, being so high and mighty. And he had more sense than you anyway. He told you more than once that the most dangerous of these spies was still loose, and you wouldn't listen. And you won't listen now. Gorbag was right, I tell you. There's a great fighter about, one of those bloody-handed Elves, or one of the filthy *tarks*.* He's coming here, I tell you. You heard the bell. He's got past the Watchers, and that's *tark*'s work. He's on the stairs. And until he's off them, I'm not going down. Not if you were a Nazgûl, I wouldn't.'

'So that's it, is it?' yelled Shagrat. 'You'll do this, and you'll not do that? And when he does come, you'll bolt and leave me? No, you won't! I'll put red maggot-holes in your belly first.'

Out of the turret-door the smaller orc came flying. Behind him came Shagrat, a large orc with long arms that, as he ran crouching, reached to the ground. But one arm hung limp and seemed to be bleeding; the other hugged a large black bundle. In the red glare Sam, cowering behind the stair-door, caught a glimpse of his evil face as it passed: it was scored as if by rending claws and smeared with blood; slaver dripped from its protruding fangs; the mouth snarled like an animal.

As far as Sam could see, Shagrat hunted Snaga round the

* See Appendix F, 139.

roof, until ducking and eluding him the smaller orc with a yelp darted back into the turret and disappeared. Then Shagrat halted. Out of the eastward door Sam could see him now by the parapet, panting, his left claw clenching and unclenching feebly. He put the bundle on the floor and with his right claw drew out a long red knife and spat on it. Going to the parapet he leaned over, looking down into the outer court far below. Twice he shouted but no answer came.

Suddenly, as Shagrat was stooped over the battlement, his back to the roof-top, Sam to his amazement saw that one of the sprawling bodies was moving. It was crawling. It put out a claw and clutched the bundle. It staggered up. In its other hand it held a broad-headed spear with a short broken haft. It was poised for a stabbing thrust. But at that very moment a hiss escaped its teeth, a gasp of pain or hate. Quick as a snake Shagrat slipped aside, twisted round, and drove his knife into his enemy's throat.

'Got you, Gorbag!' he cried. 'Not quite dead, eh? Well, I'll finish my job now.' He sprang on to the fallen body, and stamped and trampled it in his fury, stooping now and again to stab and slash it with his knife. Satisfied at last, he threw back his head and let out a horrible gurgling yell of triumph. Then he licked his knife, and put it between his teeth, and catching up the bundle he came loping towards the near door of the stairs.

Sam had no time to think. He might have slipped out of the other door, but hardly without being seen; and he could not have played hide-and-seek with this hideous orc for long. He did what was probably the best thing he could have done. He sprang out to meet Shagrat with a shout. He was no longer holding the Ring, but it was there, a hidden power, a cowing menace to the slaves of Mordor; and in his hand was Sting, and its light smote the eyes of the orc like the glitter of cruel stars in the terrible elf-countries, the dream of which was a cold fear to all his kind. And Shagrat could not both fight and keep hold of his treasure. He stopped, growling, baring his fangs. Then once more, orc-fashion, he leapt aside, and as Sam sprang at him, using the heavy bundle as both shield and weapon, he thrust it hard into his enemy's face. Sam staggered, and before he could recover, Shagrat darted past and down the stairs.

Sam ran after him, cursing, but he did not go far. Soon the thought of Frodo returned to him, and he remembered that the other orc had gone back into the turret. Here was another dreadful choice, and he had no time to ponder it. If Shagrat got away, he would soon get help and come back. But if Sam pursued him, the other orc might do some horrible deed up there. And anyway Sam might miss Shagrat or be killed by him. He turned quickly and ran back up the stairs. 'Wrong again, I expect,' he sighed. 'But it's my job to go right up to the top first, whatever happens afterwards.'

Away below Shagrat went leaping down the stairs and out over the court and through the gate, bearing his precious burden. If Sam could have seen him and known the grief that his escape would bring, he might have quailed. But now his mind was set on the last stage of his search. He came cautiously to the turret-door and stepped inside. It opened into darkness. But soon his staring eyes were aware of a dim light at his right hand. It came from an opening that led to another stairway, dark and narrow: it appeared to go winding up the turret along the inside of its round outer wall. A torch was glimmering from somewhere up above.

Softly Sam began to climb. He came to the guttering torch, fixed above a door on his left that faced a window-slit looking out westward: one of the red eyes that he and Frodo had seen from down below by the tunnel's mouth. Quickly Sam passed the door and hurried on to the second storey, dreading at any moment to be attacked and to feel throttling fingers seize his throat from behind. He came next to a window looking east and another torch above the door to a passage through the middle of the turret. The door was open, the passage dark save for the glimmer of the torch and the red glare from outside filtering through the window-slit. But here the stair stopped and climbed no further. Sam crept into the passage. On either side there was a low door; both were closed and locked. There was no sound at all.

'A dead end,' muttered Sam; 'and after all my climb! This can't be the top of the tower. But what can I do now?'

He ran back to the lower storey and tried the door. It would not move. He ran up again, and sweat began to trickle down his face. He felt that even minutes were precious, but one by one they escaped; and he could do nothing. He cared no longer for Shagrat or Snaga or any other orc that was ever spawned. He longed only for his master, for one sight of his face or one touch of his hand.

At last, weary and feeling finally defeated, he sat on a step below the level of the passage-floor and bowed his head into his hands. It was quiet, horribly quiet. The torch, that was already burning low when he arrived, sputtered and went out; and he felt the darkness cover him like a tide. And then softly, to his own surprise, there at the vain end of his long journey and his grief, moved by what thought in his heart he could not tell, Sam began to sing.

His voice sounded thin and quavering in the cold dark tower: the voice of a forlorn and weary hobbit that no listening orc could possibly mistake for the clear song of an Elven-lord. He murmured old childish tunes out of the Shire, and snatches of Mr. Bilbo's rhymes that came into his mind like fleeting glimpses of the country of his home. And then suddenly new strength rose in him, and his voice rang out, while words of his own came unbidden to fit the simple tune.

> *In western lands beneath the Sun*
> *the flowers may rise in Spring,*
> *the trees may bud, the waters run,*
> *the merry finches sing.*
> *Or there maybe 'tis cloudless night*
> *and swaying beeches bear*
> *the Elven-stars as jewels white*
> *amid their branching hair.*

Though here at journey's end I lie
  in darkness buried deep,
beyond all towers strong and high,
  beyond all mountains steep,
above all shadows rides the Sun
  and Stars for ever dwell:
I will not say the Day is done,
  nor bid the Stars farewell.

'Beyond all towers strong and high,' he began again, and then he stopped short. He thought that he had heard a faint voice answering him. But now he could hear nothing. Yes, he could hear something, but not a voice. Footsteps were approaching. Now a door was being opened quietly in the passage above; the hinges creaked. Sam crouched down listening. The door closed with a dull thud; and then a snarling orc-voice rang out.

'Ho la! You up there, you dunghill rat! Stop your squeaking, or I'll come and deal with you. D'you hear?'

There was no answer.

'All right,' growled Snaga. 'But I'll come and have a look at you all the same, and see what you're up to.'

The hinges creaked again, and Sam, now peering over the corner of the passage-threshold, saw a flicker of light in an open doorway, and the dim shape of an orc coming out. He seemed to be carrying a ladder. Suddenly the answer dawned on Sam: the topmost chamber was reached by a trap-door in the roof of the passage. Snaga thrust the ladder upwards, steadied it, and then clambered out of sight. Sam heard a bolt drawn back. Then he heard the hideous voice speaking again.

'You lie quiet, or you'll pay for it! You've not got long to live in peace, I guess; but if you don't want the fun to begin right now, keep your trap shut, see? There's a reminder for you!' There was a sound like the crack of a whip.

At that rage blazed in Sam's heart to a sudden fury. He sprang up, ran, and went up the ladder like a cat. His head came out in the middle of the floor of a large round chamber. A red lamp hung from its roof; the westward window-slit was high and dark. Something was lying on the floor by the wall under the window, but over it a black orc-shape was straddled. It raised a whip a second time, but the blow never fell.

With a cry Sam leapt across the floor, Sting in hand. The orc wheeled round, but before it could make a move Sam slashed its whip-hand from its arm. Howling with pain and fear but desperate the orc charged head-down at him. Sam's next blow went wide, and thrown off his balance he fell backwards, clutching at the orc as it stumbled over him. Before he could scramble up he heard a cry and a thud. The orc in its wild haste had tripped on the ladder-head and fallen through the open trap-door. Sam gave no more thought to it. He ran to the figure huddled on the floor. It was Frodo.

He was naked, lying as if in a swoon on a heap of filthy rags: his arm was flung up, shielding his head, and across his side there ran an ugly whip-weal.

'Frodo! Mr. Frodo, my dear!' cried Sam, tears almost blinding him. 'It's Sam, I've come!' He half lifted his master and hugged him to his breast. Frodo opened his eyes.

'Am I still dreaming?' he muttered. 'But the other dreams were horrible.'

'You're not dreaming at all, Master,' said Sam. 'It's real. It's me. I've come.'

'I can hardly believe it,' said Frodo, clutching him. 'There was an orc with a whip, and then it turns into Sam! Then I wasn't dreaming after all when I heard that singing down below, and I tried to answer? Was it you?'

'It was indeed, Mr. Frodo. I'd given up hope, almost. I couldn't find you.'

'Well, you have now, Sam, dear Sam,' said Frodo, and he lay back in Sam's gentle arms, closing his eyes, like a child at rest when night-fears are driven away by some loved voice or hand.

Sam felt that he could sit like that in endless happiness; but it was not allowed. It was not enough for him to find his master, he had still to try and save him. He kissed Frodo's forehead. 'Come! Wake up, Mr. Frodo!' he said, trying to sound as cheerful as he had when he drew back the curtains at Bag End on a summer's morning.

Frodo sighed and sat up. 'Where are we? How did I get here?' he asked.

'There's no time for tales till we get somewhere else, Mr. Frodo,' said Sam. 'But you're in the top of that tower you and me saw from away down by the tunnel before the orcs got you. How long ago that was I don't know. More than a day, I guess.'

'Only that?' said Frodo. 'It seems weeks. You must tell me all about it, if we get a chance. Something hit me, didn't it? And I fell into darkness and foul dreams, and woke and found that waking was worse. Orcs were all round me. I think they had just been pouring some horrible burning drink down my throat. My head grew clear, but I was aching and weary. They stripped me of everything; and then two great brutes came and questioned me, questioned me until I thought I should go mad, standing over me, gloating, fingering their knives. I'll never forget their claws and eyes.'

'You won't, if you talk about them, Mr. Frodo,' said Sam. 'And if we don't want to see them again, the sooner we get going the better. Can you walk?'

'Yes, I can walk,' said Frodo, getting up slowly. 'I am not hurt, Sam. Only I feel very tired, and I've a pain here.' He put his hand to the back of his neck above his left shoulder. He stood up, and it looked to Sam as if he was clothed in flame: his naked skin was scarlet in the light of the lamp above. Twice he paced across the floor.

'That's better!' he said, his spirits rising a little. 'I didn't dare to move when I was left alone, or one of the guards came. Until the yelling and fighting began. The two big brutes: they quarrelled, I think. Over me and my things. I lay here terrified. And then all went deadly quiet, and that was worse.'

'Yes, they quarrelled, seemingly,' said Sam. 'There must have been a couple of hundred of the dirty creatures in this place. A bit of a tall order for Sam Gamgee, as you might say. But they've done all the killing of themselves. That's lucky, but it's too long to make a song about, till we're out of here. Now what's to be done? You can't go walking in the Black Land in naught but your skin, Mr. Frodo.'

'They've taken everything, Sam,' said Frodo. 'Everything I had. Do you understand? *Everything!*' He cowered on the floor again with bowed head, as his own words brought home to him the fullness of the disaster, and despair overwhelmed him. 'The quest has failed, Sam. Even if we get out of here, we can't escape. Only Elves can escape. Away, away out of Middle-earth, far away over the Sea. If even that is wide enough to keep the Shadow out.'

'No, *not* everything, Mr. Frodo. And it hasn't failed, not yet. I took it, Mr. Frodo, begging your pardon. And I've kept it safe. It's round my neck now, and a terrible burden it is, too.' Sam fumbled for the Ring and its chain. 'But I suppose you must take it back.' Now it had come to it, Sam felt reluctant to give up the Ring and burden his master with it again.

'You've got it?' gasped Frodo. 'You've got it here? Sam, you're a marvel!' Then quickly and strangely his tone changed. 'Give it to me!' he cried, standing up, holding out a trembling hand. 'Give it me at once! You can't have it!'

'All right, Mr. Frodo,' said Sam, rather startled. 'Here it is!' Slowly he drew the Ring out and passed the chain over his head. 'But you're in the land of Mordor now, sir; and when you get out, you'll see the Fiery Mountain and all. You'll find the Ring very dangerous now, and very hard to bear. If it's too hard a job, I could share it with you, maybe?'

'No, no!' cried Frodo, snatching the Ring and chain from Sam's hands. 'No you won't, you thief!' He panted, staring at Sam with eyes wide with fear and enmity. Then suddenly, clasping the Ring in one clenched fist, he stood aghast. A mist seemed to clear from his eyes, and he passed a hand over his aching brow. The hideous vision had seemed so real to him, half bemused as he was still with wound and fear. Sam had changed before his very eyes into an orc again, leering and pawing at his treasure, a foul little creature with greedy eyes and slobbering mouth. But now the vision had passed. There was Sam kneeling before him, his face wrung with pain, as if he had been stabbed in the heart; tears welled from his eyes.

'O Sam!' cried Frodo. 'What have I said? What have I done? Forgive me! After all you have done. It is the horrible power of the Ring. I wish it had never, never, been found. But don't mind me, Sam. I must carry the burden to the end. It can't be altered. You can't come between me and this doom.'

'That's all right, Mr. Frodo,' said Sam, rubbing his sleeve across his eyes. 'I understand. But I can still help, can't I? I've got to get you out of here. At once, see! But first you want some clothes and gear, and then some food. The clothes will be the easiest part. As we're in Mordor, we'd best dress up Mordor-fashion; and anyway there isn't no choice. It'll have to be orc-stuff for you, Mr. Frodo, I'm afraid. And for me too. If we go together, we'd best match. Now put this round you!'

Sam unclasped his grey cloak and cast it about Frodo's shoulders. Then unslinging his pack he laid it on the floor. He drew Sting from its sheath. Hardly a flicker was to be seen upon its blade. 'I was forgetting this, Mr. Frodo,' he said. 'No, they didn't get everything! You lent me Sting, if you remember, and the Lady's glass. I've got them both still. But lend them to me a little longer, Mr. Frodo. I must go and see what I can find. You stay here. Walk about a bit and ease your legs. I shan't be long. I shan't have to go far.'

'Take care, Sam!' said Frodo. 'And be quick! There may be orcs still alive, lurking in wait.'

'I've got to chance it,' said Sam. He stepped to the trap-door and slipped down the ladder. In a minute his head reappeared. He threw a long knife on the floor.

'There's something that might be useful,' he said. 'He's dead: the one that whipped you. Broke his neck, it seems, in his hurry. Now you draw up the ladder, if you can, Mr. Frodo; and don't you let it down till you hear me call the pass-word. *Elbereth* I'll call. What the Elves say. No orc would say that.'

Frodo sat for a while and shivered, dreadful fears chasing one another through his mind. Then he got up, drew the grey elven-cloak about him, and to keep his mind occupied, began to walk to and fro, prying and peering into every corner of his prison.

It was not very long, though fear made it seem an hour at least, before he heard Sam's voice calling softly from below: *Elbereth, Elbereth*. Frodo let down the light ladder. Up came Sam, puffing, heaving a great bundle on his head. He let it fall with a thud.

'Quick now, Mr. Frodo!' he said. 'I've had a bit of a search to find anything small enough for the likes of us. We'll have to make do. But we must hurry. I've met nothing alive, and I've seen nothing, but I'm not easy. I think this place is being watched. I can't explain it, but well: it feels to me as if one of those foul flying Riders was about, up in the blackness where he can't be seen.'

He opened the bundle. Frodo looked in disgust at the contents, but there was nothing for it: he had to put the things on, or go naked. There were long hairy breeches of some unclean beast-fell, and a tunic of dirty leather. He drew them on. Over the tunic went a coat of stout ring-mail, short for a full-sized orc, too long for Frodo and heavy. About it he clasped a belt, at which there hung a short sheath holding a broad-bladed stabbing-sword. Sam had brought several orc-helmets. One of them fitted Frodo well enough, a black cap with iron rim, and iron hoops covered with leather upon which the Evil Eye was painted in red above the beaklike nose-guard.

'The Morgul-stuff, Gorbag's gear, was a better fit and

better made,' said Sam; 'but it wouldn't do, I guess, to go carrying his tokens into Mordor, not after this business here. Well, there you are, Mr. Frodo. A perfect little orc, if I may make so bold – at least you would be, if we could cover your face with a mask, give you longer arms, and make you bow-legged. This will hide some of the tell-tales.' He put a large black cloak round Frodo's shoulders. 'Now you're ready! You can pick up a shield as we go.'

'What about you, Sam?' said Frodo. 'Aren't we going to match?'

'Well, Mr. Frodo, I've been thinking,' said Sam. 'I'd best not leave any of my stuff behind, and we can't destroy it. And I can't wear orc-mail over all my clothes, can I? I'll just have to cover up.'

He knelt down and carefully folded his elven-cloak. It went into a surprisingly small roll. This he put into his pack that lay on the floor. Standing up, he slung it behind his back, put an orc-helm on his head, and cast another black cloak about his shoulders. 'There!' he said. 'Now we match, near enough. And now we must be off!'

'I can't go all the way at a run, Sam,' said Frodo with a wry smile. 'I hope you've made inquiries about inns along the road? Or have you forgotten about food and drink?'

'Save me, but so I had!' said Sam. He whistled in dismay. 'Bless me, Mr. Frodo, but you've gone and made me that hungry and thirsty! I don't know when drop or morsel last passed my lips. I'd forgotten it, trying to find you. But let me think! Last time I looked I'd got about enough of that waybread, and of what Captain Faramir gave us, to keep me on my legs for a couple of weeks at a pinch. But if there's a drop left in my bottle, there's no more. That's not going to be enough for two, nohow. Don't orcs eat, and don't they drink? Or do they just live on foul air and poison?'

'No, they eat and drink, Sam. The Shadow that bred them can only mock, it cannot make: not real new things of its own. I don't think it gave life to the orcs, it only ruined them and twisted them; and if they are to live at all, they have to live like other living creatures. Foul waters and foul meats they'll take, if they can get no better, but not poison. They've fed me, and so I'm better off than you. There must be food and water somewhere in this place.'

'But there's no time to look for them,' said Sam.

'Well, things are a bit better than you think,' said Frodo. 'I have had a bit of luck while you were away. Indeed they did not take everything. I've found my food-bag among some rags on the floor. They've rummaged it, of course. But I guess they disliked the very look and smell of the *lembas*, worse than Gollum did. It's scattered about and some of it is trampled and broken, but I've gathered it together. It's not far short of what you've got. But they've taken Faramir's food, and they've slashed up my water-bottle.'

'Well, there's no more to be said,' said Sam. 'We've got enough to start on. But the water's going to be a bad business. But come, Mr. Frodo! Off we go, or a whole lake of it won't do us any good!'

'Not till you've had a mouthful, Sam,' said Frodo. 'I won't budge. Here, take this elven-cake, and drink that last drop in your bottle! The whole thing is quite hopeless, so it's no good worrying about tomorrow. It probably won't come.'

At last they started. Down the ladder they climbed, and then Sam took it and laid it in the passage beside the huddled body of the fallen orc. The stair was dark, but on the roof-top the glare of the Mountain could still be seen, though it was dying down now to a sullen red. They picked up two shields to complete their disguise and then went on.

Down the great stairway they plodded. The high chamber of the turret behind, where they had met again, seemed almost homely: they were out in the open again now, and terror ran along the walls. All might be dead in the Tower of Cirith Ungol, but it was steeped in fear and evil still.

At length they came to the door upon the outer court, and they halted. Even from where they stood they felt the malice of the Watchers beating on them, black silent shapes on either side of the gate through which the glare of Mordor dimly showed. As they threaded their way among the hideous bodies of the orcs each step became more difficult. Before they even reached the archway they were brought to a stand. To move an inch further was a pain and weariness to will and limb.

Frodo had no strength for such a battle. He sank to the ground. 'I can't go on, Sam,' he murmured. 'I'm going to faint. I don't know what's come over me.'

'I do, Mr. Frodo. Hold up now! It's the gate. There's some devilry there. But I got through, and I'm going to get out. It can't be more dangerous than before. Now for it!'

Sam drew out the elven-glass of Galadriel again. As if to do honour to his hardihood, and to grace with splendour his faithful brown hobbit-hand that had done such deeds, the phial blazed forth suddenly, so that all the shadowy court was lit with a dazzling radiance like lightning; but it remained steady and did not pass.

'*Gilthoniel, A Elbereth!*' Sam cried. For, why he did not know, his thought sprang back suddenly to the Elves in the Shire, and the song that drove away the Black Rider in the trees.

'*Aiya elenion ancalima!*' cried Frodo once again behind him.

The will of the Watchers was broken with a suddenness like the snapping of a cord, and Frodo and Sam stumbled forward. Then they ran. Through the gate and past the great seated figures with their glittering eyes. There was a crack. The keystone of the arch crashed almost on their heels, and the wall above crumbled, and fell in ruin. Only by a hair did they escape. A bell clanged; and from the Watchers there went up a high and dreadful wail. Far up above in the darkness it was answered. Out of the black sky there came dropping like a bolt a winged shape, rending the clouds with a ghastly shriek.

CHAPTER II

THE LAND OF SHADOW

Sam had just wits enough left to thrust the phial back into his breast. 'Run, Mr. Frodo!' he cried. 'No, not that way! There's a sheer drop over the wall. Follow me!'

Down the road from the gate they fled. In fifty paces, with a swift bend round a jutting bastion of the cliff, it took them out of sight from the Tower. They had escaped for the moment. Cowering back against the rock they drew breath, and then they clutched at their hearts. Perching now on the wall beside the ruined gate the Nazgûl sent out its deadly cries. All the cliffs echoed.

In terror they stumbled on. Soon the road bent sharply eastward again and exposed them for a dreadful moment to view from the Tower. As they flitted across they glanced back and saw the great black shape upon the battlement; then they plunged down between high rock-walls in a cutting that fell steeply to join the Morgul-road. They came to the way-meeting. There was still no sign of orcs, nor of an answer to the cry of the Nazgûl; but they knew that the silence would not last long. At any moment now the hunt would begin.

'This won't do, Sam,' said Frodo. 'If we were real orcs, we ought to be dashing back to the Tower, not running away. The first enemy we meet will know us. We must get off this road somehow.'

'But we can't,' said Sam, 'not without wings.'

The eastern faces of the Ephel Dúath were sheer, falling in cliff and precipice to the black trough that lay between them and the inner ridge. A short way beyond the way-meeting, after another steep incline, a flying bridge of stone leapt over the chasm and bore the road across into the

tumbled slopes and glens of the Morgai. With a desperate
spurt Frodo and Sam dashed along the bridge; but they had
hardly reached its further end when they heard the hue and
cry begin. Away behind them, now high above on the mountain-side, loomed the Tower of Cirith Ungol, its stones glowing dully. Suddenly its harsh bell clanged again, and then
broke into a shattering peal. Horns sounded. And now from
beyond the bridge-end came answering cries. Down in the
dark trough, cut off from the dying glare of Orodruin, Frodo
and Sam could not see ahead, but already they heard the
tramp of iron-shod feet, and upon the road there rang the
swift clatter of hoofs.

'Quick, Sam! Over we go!' cried Frodo. They scrambled
on to the low parapet of the bridge. Fortunately there was
no longer any dreadful drop into the gulf, for the slopes of
the Morgai had already risen almost to the level of the road;
but it was too dark for them to guess the depth of the fall.

'Well, here goes, Mr. Frodo,' said Sam. 'Good-bye!'

He let go. Frodo followed. And even as they fell they heard
the rush of horsemen sweeping over the bridge and the rattle
of orc-feet running up behind. But Sam would have laughed,
if he had dared. Half fearing a breaking plunge down on to
unseen rocks the hobbits landed, in a drop of no more than
a dozen feet, with a thud and a crunch into the last thing
that they had expected: a tangle of thorny bushes. There
Sam lay still, softly sucking a scratched hand.

When the sound of hoof and foot had passed he ventured
a whisper. 'Bless me, Mr. Frodo, but I didn't know as anything grew in Mordor! But if I had a'known, this is just what
I'd have looked for. These thorns must be a foot long by the
feel of them; they've stuck through everything I've got on.
Wish I'd a'put that mailshirt on!'

'Orc-mail doesn't keep these thorns out,' said Frodo. 'Not
even a leather jerkin is any good.'

They had a struggle to get out of the thicket. The thorns
and briars were as tough as wire and as clinging as claws.

Their cloaks were rent and tattered before they broke free at last.

'Now down we go, Sam,' Frodo whispered. 'Down into the valley quick, and then turn northward, as soon as ever we can.'

Day was coming again in the world outside, and far beyond the glooms of Mordor the Sun was climbing over the eastern rim of Middle-earth; but here all was still dark as night. The Mountain smouldered and its fires went out. The glare faded from the cliffs. The easterly wind that had been blowing ever since they left Ithilien now seemed dead. Slowly and painfully they clambered down, groping, stumbling, scrambling among rock and briar and dead wood in the blind shadows, down and down until they could go no further.

At length they stopped, and sat side by side, their backs against a boulder. Both were sweating. 'If Shagrat himself was to offer me a glass of water, I'd shake his hand,' said Sam.

'Don't say such things!' said Frodo. 'It only makes it worse.' Then he stretched himself out, dizzy and weary, and he spoke no more for a while. At last with a struggle he got up again. To his amazement he found that Sam was asleep. 'Wake up, Sam!' he said. 'Come on! It's time we made another effort.'

Sam scrambled to his feet. 'Well I never!' he said. 'I must have dropped off. It's a long time, Mr. Frodo, since I had a proper sleep, and my eyes just closed down on their own.'

Frodo now led the way, northward as near as he could guess, among the stones and boulders lying thick at the bottom of the great ravine. But presently he stopped again.

'It's no good, Sam,' he said. 'I can't manage it. This mail-shirt, I mean. Not in my present state. Even my mithril-coat seemed heavy when I was tired. This is far heavier. And what's the use of it? We shan't win through by fighting.'

'But we may have some to do,' said Sam. 'And there's

knives and stray arrows. That Gollum isn't dead, for one thing. I don't like to think of you with naught but a bit of leather between you and a stab in the dark.'

'Look here, Sam dear lad,' said Frodo: 'I am tired, weary, I haven't a hope left. But I have to go on trying to get to the Mountain, as long as I can move. The Ring is enough. This extra weight is killing me. It must go. But don't think I'm ungrateful. I hate to think of the foul work you must have had among the bodies to find it for me.'

'Don't talk about it, Mr. Frodo. Bless you! I'd carry you on my back, if I could. Let it go then!'

Frodo laid aside his cloak and took off the orc-mail and flung it away. He shivered a little. 'What I really need is something warm,' he said. 'It's gone cold, or else I've caught a chill.'

'You can have my cloak, Mr. Frodo,' said Sam. He unslung his pack and took out the elven-cloak. 'How's this, Mr. Frodo?' he said. 'You wrap that orc-rag close round you, and put the belt outside it. Then this can go over all. It don't look quite orc-fashion, but it'll keep you warmer; and I daresay it'll keep you from harm better than any other gear. It was made by the Lady.'

Frodo took the cloak and fastened the brooch. 'That's better!' he said. 'I feel much lighter. I can go on now. But this blind dark seems to be getting into my heart. As I lay in prison, Sam, I tried to remember the Brandywine, and Woody End, and The Water running through the mill at Hobbiton. But I can't see them now.'

'There now, Mr. Frodo, it's you that's talking of water this time!' said Sam. 'If only the Lady could see us or hear us, I'd say to her: "Your Ladyship, all we want is light and water: just clean water and plain daylight, better than any jewels, begging your pardon." But it's a long way to Lórien.' Sam sighed and waved his hand towards the heights of the Ephel Dúath, now only to be guessed as a deeper blackness against the black sky.

* * *

They started off again. They had not gone far when Frodo paused. 'There's a Black Rider over us,' he said. 'I can feel it. We had better keep still for a while.'

Crouched under a great boulder they sat facing back west-ward and did not speak for some time. Then Frodo breathed a sigh of relief. 'It's passed,' he said. They stood up, and then they both stared in wonder. Away to their left, south-ward, against a sky that was turning grey, the peaks and high ridges of the great range began to appear dark and black, visible shapes. Light was growing behind them. Slowly it crept towards the North. There was battle far above in the high spaces of the air. The billowing clouds of Mordor were being driven back, their edges tattering as a wind out of the living world came up and swept the fumes and smokes towards the dark land of their home. Under the lifting skirts of the dreary canopy dim light leaked into Mordor like pale morning through the grimed window of a prison.

'Look at it, Mr. Frodo!' said Sam. 'Look at it! The wind's changed. Something's happening. He's not having it all his own way. His darkness is breaking up out in the world there. I wish I could see what is going on!'

It was the morning of the fifteenth of March, and over the Vale of Anduin the Sun was rising above the eastern shadow, and the south-west wind was blowing. Théoden lay dying on the Pelennor Fields.

As Frodo and Sam stood and gazed, the rim of light spread all along the line of the Ephel Dúath, and then they saw a shape, moving at a great speed out of the West, at first only a black speck against the glimmering strip above the moun-tain-tops, but growing, until it plunged like a bolt into the dark canopy and passed high above them. As it went it sent out a long shrill cry, the voice of a Nazgûl; but this cry no longer held any terror for them: it was a cry of woe and dismay, ill tidings for the Dark Tower. The Lord of the Ringwraiths had met his doom.

'What did I tell you? Something's happening!' cried Sam. ' "The war's going well," said Shagrat; but Gorbag he wasn't so sure. And he was right there too. Things are looking up, Mr. Frodo. Haven't you got some hope now?'

'Well no, not much, Sam,' Frodo sighed. 'That's away beyond the mountains. We're going east not west. And I'm so tired. And the Ring is so heavy, Sam. And I begin to see it in my mind all the time, like a great wheel of fire.'

Sam's quick spirits sank again at once. He looked at his master anxiously, and he took his hand. 'Come, Mr. Frodo!' he said. 'I've got one thing I wanted: a bit of light. Enough to help us, and yet I guess it's dangerous too. Try a bit further, and then we'll lie close and have a rest. But take a morsel to eat now, a bit of the Elves' food; it may hearten you.'

Sharing a wafer of *lembas*, and munching it as best they could with their parched mouths, Frodo and Sam plodded on. The light, though no more than a grey dusk, was now enough for them to see that they were deep in the valley between the mountains. It sloped up gently northward, and at its bottom went the bed of a now dry and withered stream. Beyond its stony course they saw a beaten path that wound its way under the feet of the westward cliffs. Had they known, they could have reached it quicker, for it was a track that left the main Morgul-road at the western bridge-end and went down by a long stair cut in the rock to the valley's bottom. It was used by patrols or by messengers going swiftly to lesser posts and strongholds north-away, between Cirith Ungol and the narrows of Isenmouthe, the iron jaws of Carach Angren.

It was perilous for the hobbits to use such a path, but they needed speed, and Frodo felt that he could not face the toil of scrambling among the boulders or in the trackless glens of the Morgai. And he judged that northward was, maybe, the way that their hunters would least expect them to take. The road east to the plain, or the pass back westward, those they would first search most thoroughly. Only when he was well north of the Tower did he mean to turn and seek for some way to take him east, east on the last desperate stage of his journey. So now they crossed the stony bed and took to the orc-path, and for some time they marched along it. The cliffs at their left were overhung, and they could not be seen from above; but the path made many bends, and at each bend they gripped their sword-hilts and went forward cautiously.

The light grew no stronger, for Orodruin was still belching forth a great fume that, beaten upwards by the opposing airs, mounted higher and higher, until it reached a region above the wind and spread in an immeasurable roof, whose central pillar rose out of the shadows beyond their view. They had trudged for more than an hour when they heard a sound that brought them to a halt. Unbelievable, but unmistakable. Water trickling. Out of a gully on the left, so sharp and narrow that it looked as if the black cliff had been cloven by some huge axe, water came dripping down: the last remains, maybe, of some sweet rain gathered from sunlit seas, but ill-fated to fall at last upon the walls of the Black Land and wander fruitless down into the dust. Here it came out of the rock in a little falling streamlet, and flowed across the path, and turning south ran away swiftly to be lost among the dead stones.

Sam sprang towards it. 'If ever I see the Lady again, I will tell her!' he cried. 'Light and now water!' Then he stopped. 'Let me drink first, Mr. Frodo,' he said.

'All right, but there's room enough for two.'

'I didn't mean that,' said Sam. 'I mean: if it's poisonous, or something that will show its badness quick, well, better me than you, master, if you understand me.'

'I do. But I think we'll trust our luck together, Sam; or our blessing. Still, be careful now, if it's very cold!'

The water was cool but not icy, and it had an unpleasant taste, at once bitter and oily, or so they would have said at home. Here it seemed beyond all praise, and beyond fear or prudence. They drank their fill, and Sam replenished his water-bottle. After that Frodo felt easier, and they went on for several miles, until the broadening of the road and the beginnings of a rough wall along its edge warned them that they were drawing near to another orc-hold.

'This is where we turn aside, Sam,' said Frodo. 'And we must turn east.' He sighed as he looked at the gloomy ridges across the valley. 'I have just about enough strength left to find some hole away up there. And then I must rest a little.'

The river-bed was now some way below the path. They scrambled down to it, and began to cross it. To their surprise they came upon dark pools fed by threads of water trickling down from some source higher up the valley. Upon its outer marges under the westward mountains Mordor was a dying land, but it was not yet dead. And here things still grew, harsh, twisted, bitter, struggling for life. In the glens of the Morgai on the other side of the valley low scrubby trees lurked and clung, coarse grey grass-tussocks fought with the stones, and withered mosses crawled on them; and everywhere great writhing, tangled brambles sprawled. Some had long stabbing thorns, some hooked barbs that rent like knives. The sullen shrivelled leaves of a past year hung on them, grating and rattling in the sad airs, but their maggot-ridden buds were only just opening. Flies, dun or grey, or black, marked like orcs with a red eye-shaped blotch, buzzed and stung; and above the briar-thickets clouds of hungry midges danced and reeled.

'Orc-gear's no good,' said Sam waving his arms. 'I wish I'd got an orc's hide!'

At last Frodo could go no further. They had climbed up a narrow shelving ravine, but they still had a long way to go before they could even come in sight of the last craggy ridge. 'I must rest now, Sam, and sleep if I can,' said Frodo. He looked about, but there seemed nowhere even for an animal to crawl into in this dismal country. At length, tired out, they slunk under a curtain of brambles that hung down like a mat over a low rock-face.

There they sat and made such a meal as they could. Keeping back the precious *lembas* for the evil days ahead, they ate

the half of what remained in Sam's bag of Faramir's provision: some dried fruit, and a small slip of cured meat; and
they sipped some water. They had drunk again from the
pools in the valley, but they were very thirsty again. There
was a bitter tang in the air of Mordor that dried the mouth.
When Sam thought of water even his hopeful spirit quailed.
Beyond the Morgai there was the dreadful plain of Gorgoroth
to cross.

'Now you go to sleep first, Mr. Frodo,' he said. 'It's getting
dark again. I reckon this day is nearly over.'

Frodo sighed and was asleep almost before the words were
spoken. Sam struggled with his own weariness, and he took
Frodo's hand; and there he sat silent till deep night fell. Then
at last, to keep himself awake, he crawled from the hiding-
place and looked out. The land seemed full of creaking and
cracking and sly noises, but there was no sound of voice or
of foot. Far above the Ephel Dúath in the West the night-sky
was still dim and pale. There, peeping among the cloud-
wrack above a dark tor high up in the mountains, Sam saw
a white star twinkle for a while. The beauty of it smote his
heart, as he looked up out of the forsaken land, and hope
returned to him. For like a shaft, clear and cold, the thought
pierced him that in the end the Shadow was only a small and
passing thing: there was light and high beauty for ever beyond
its reach. His song in the Tower had been defiance rather
than hope; for then he was thinking of himself. Now, for a
moment, his own fate, and even his master's, ceased to
trouble him. He crawled back into the brambles and laid
himself by Frodo's side, and putting away all fear he cast
himself into a deep untroubled sleep.

They woke together, hand in hand. Sam was almost fresh,
ready for another day; but Frodo sighed. His sleep had been
uneasy, full of dreams of fire, and waking brought him no
comfort. Still his sleep had not been without all healing virtue:
he was stronger, more able to bear his burden one stage
further. They did not know the time, nor how long they had

slept; but after a morsel of food and a sip of water they went
on up the ravine, until it ended in a sharp slope of screes
and sliding stones. There the last living things gave up their
struggle; the tops of the Morgai were grassless, bare, jagged,
barren as a slate.

After much wandering and search they found a way that
they could climb, and with a last hundred feet of clawing
scramble they were up. They came to a cleft between two
dark crags, and passing through found themselves on the
very edge of the last fence of Mordor. Below them, at the
bottom of a fall of some fifteen hundred feet, lay the inner
plain stretching away into a formless gloom beyond their
sight. The wind of the world blew now from the West, and
the great clouds were lifted high, floating away eastward; but
still only a grey light came to the dreary fields of Gorgoroth.
There smokes trailed on the ground and lurked in hollows,
and fumes leaked from fissures in the earth.

Still far away, forty miles at least, they saw Mount Doom,
its feet founded in ashen ruin, its huge cone rising to a great
height, where its reeking head was swathed in cloud. Its fires
were now dimmed, and it stood in smouldering slumber, as
threatening and dangerous as a sleeping beast. Behind it there
hung a vast shadow, ominous as a thunder-cloud, the veils
of Barad-dûr that was reared far away upon a long spur of
the Ashen Mountains thrust down from the North. The Dark
Power was deep in thought, and the Eye turned inward,
pondering tidings of doubt and danger: a bright sword, and
a stern and kingly face it saw, and for a while it gave little
thought to other things; and all its great stronghold, gate on
gate, and tower on tower, was wrapped in a brooding
gloom.

Frodo and Sam gazed out in mingled loathing and wonder
on this hateful land. Between them and the smoking mountain, and about it north and south, all seemed ruinous and
dead, a desert burned and choked. They wondered how the
Lord of this realm maintained and fed his slaves and his
armies. Yet armies he had. As far as their eyes could reach,

along the skirts of the Morgai and away southward, there were camps, some of tents, some ordered like small towns. One of the largest of these was right below them. Barely a mile out into the plain it clustered like some huge nest of insects, with straight dreary streets of huts and long low drab buildings. About it the ground was busy with folk going to and fro; a wide road ran from it south-east to join the Morgul-way, and along it many lines of small black shapes were hurrying.

'I don't like the look of things at all,' said Sam. 'Pretty hopeless, I call it – saving that where there's such a lot of folk there must be wells or water, not to mention food. And these are Men not Orcs, or my eyes are all wrong.'

Neither he nor Frodo knew anything of the great slave-worked fields away south in this wide realm, beyond the fumes of the Mountain by the dark sad waters of Lake Núrnen; nor of the great roads that ran away east and south to tributary lands, from which the soldiers of the Tower brought long waggon-trains of goods and booty and fresh slaves. Here in the northward regions were the mines and forges, and the musterings of long-planned war; and here the Dark Power, moving its armies like pieces on the board, was gathering them together. Its first moves, the first feelers of its strength, had been checked upon its western line, south-ward and northward. For the moment it withdrew them, and brought up new forces, massing them about Cirith Gorgor for an avenging stroke. And if it had also been its purpose to defend the Mountain against all approach, it could scarcely have done more.

'Well!' Sam went on. 'Whatever they have to eat and drink, we can't get it. There's no way down that I can see. And we couldn't cross all that open country crawling with enemies, even if we did get down.'

'Still we shall have to try,' said Frodo. 'It's no worse than I expected. I never hoped to get across. I can't see any hope of it now. But I've still got to do the best I can. At present that is to avoid being captured as long as possible. So we must still go northwards, I think, and see what it is like where the open plain is narrower.'

'I guess what it'll be like,' said Sam. 'Where it's narrower the Orcs and Men will just be packed closer. You'll see, Mr. Frodo.'

'I dare say I shall, if we ever get so far,' said Frodo and turned away.

They soon found that it was impossible to make their way along the crest of the Morgai, or anywhere along its higher levels, pathless as they were and scored with deep ghylls. In the end they were forced to go back down the ravine that they had climbed and seek for a way along the valley. It was rough going, for they dared not cross over to the path on the westward side. After a mile or more they saw, huddled in a hollow at the cliff's foot, the orc-hold that they had guessed was near at hand: a wall and a cluster of stone huts set about the dark mouth of a cave. There was no movement to be seen, but the hobbits crept by cautiously, keeping as much as they could to the thorn-brakes that grew thickly at this point along both sides of the old water-course.

They went two or three miles further, and the orc-hold was hidden from sight behind them; but they had hardly begun to breathe more freely again when harsh and loud they heard orc-voices. Quickly they slunk out of sight behind a brown and stunted bush. The voices drew nearer. Presently two orcs came into view. One was clad in ragged brown and was armed with a bow of horn; it was of a small breed, black-skinned, with wide and snuffling nostrils: evidently a tracker of some kind. The other was a big fighting-orc, like those of Shagrat's company, bearing the token of the Eye. He also had a bow at his back and carried a short broad-headed spear. As usual they were quarrelling, and being of different breeds they used the Common Speech after their fashion.

Hardly twenty paces from where the hobbits lurked the small orc stopped. 'Nar!' it snarled. 'I'm going home.' It pointed across the valley to the orc-hold. 'No good wearing my nose out on stones any more. There's not a trace left, I say. I've lost the scent through giving way to you. It went up into the hills, not along the valley, I tell you.'

'Not much use are you, you little snufflers?' said the big orc. 'I reckon eyes are better than your snotty noses.'

'Then what have you seen with them?' snarled the other. 'Garn! You don't even know what you're looking for.'

'Whose blame's that?' said the soldier. 'Not mine. That comes from Higher Up. First they say it's a great Elf in bright armour, then it's a sort of small dwarf-man, then it must be a pack of rebel Uruk-hai; or maybe it's all the lot together.'

'Ar!' said the tracker. 'They've lost their heads, that's what it is. And some of the bosses are going to lose their skins too, I guess, if what I hear is true: Tower raided and all, and hundreds of your lads done in, and prisoner got away. If that's the way you fighters go on, small wonder there's bad news from the battles.'

'Who says there's bad news?' shouted the soldier.

'Ar! Who says there isn't?'

'That's cursed rebel-talk, and I'll stick you, if you don't shut it down, see?'

'All right, all right!' said the tracker. 'I'll say no more and go on thinking. But what's the black sneak got to do with it all? That gobbler with the flapping hands?'

'I don't know. Nothing, maybe. But he's up to no good, nosing around, I'll wager. Curse him! No sooner had he slipped us and run off than word came he's wanted alive, wanted quick.'

'Well, I hope they get him and put him through it,' growled the tracker. 'He messed up the scent back there, pinching that cast-off mail-shirt that he found, and paddling all round the place before I could get there.'

'It saved his life anyhow,' said the soldier. 'Why, before I knew he was wanted I shot him, as neat as neat, at fifty paces right in the back; but he ran on.'

'Garn! You missed him,' said the tracker. 'First you shoot

wild, then you run too slow, and then you send for the poor trackers. I've had enough of you.' He loped off.

'You come back,' shouted the soldier, 'or I'll report you!'

'Who to? Not to your precious Shagrat. He won't be captain any more.'

'I'll give your name and number to the Nazgûl,' said the soldier lowering his voice to a hiss. 'One of *them*'s in charge at the Tower now.'

The other halted, and his voice was full of fear and rage. 'You cursed peaching sneakthief!' he yelled. 'You can't do your job, and you can't even stick by your own folk. Go to your filthy Shriekers, and may they freeze the flesh off you! If the enemy doesn't get them first. They've done in Number One, I've heard, and I hope it's true!'

The big orc, spear in hand, leapt after him. But the tracker, springing behind a stone, put an arrow in his eye as he ran up, and he fell with a crash. The other ran off across the valley and disappeared.

For a while the hobbits sat in silence. At length Sam stirred. 'Well, I call that neat as neat,' he said. 'If this nice friendliness would spread about in Mordor, half our trouble would be over.'

'Quietly, Sam,' Frodo whispered. 'There may be others about. We have evidently had a very narrow escape, and the hunt was hotter on our tracks than we guessed. But that *is* the spirit of Mordor, Sam; and it has spread to every corner of it. Orcs have always behaved like that, or so all tales say, when they are on their own. But you can't get much hope out of it. They hate us far more, altogether and all the time. If those two had seen us, they would have dropped all their quarrel until we were dead.'

There was another long silence. Sam broke it again, but with a whisper this time. 'Did you hear what they said about *that gobbler*, Mr. Frodo? I told you Gollum wasn't dead yet, didn't I?'

'Yes, I remember. And I wondered how you knew,' said

Frodo. 'Well, come now! I think we had better not move out from here again, until it has gone quite dark. So you shall tell me how you know, and all about what happened. If you can do it quietly.'

'I'll try,' said Sam, 'but when I think of that Stinker I get so hot I could shout.'

There the hobbits sat under the cover of the thorny bush, while the drear light of Mordor faded slowly into a deep and starless night; and Sam spoke into Frodo's ear all that he could find words for of Gollum's treacherous attack, the horror of Shelob, and his own adventures with the orcs. When he had finished, Frodo said nothing but took Sam's hand and pressed it. At length he stirred.

'Well, I suppose we must be going on again,' he said. 'I wonder how long it will be before we really are caught and all the toiling and the slinking will be over, and in vain.' He stood up. 'It's dark, and we cannot use the Lady's glass. Keep it safe for me, Sam. I have nowhere to keep it now, except in my hand, and I shall need both hands in the blind night. But Sting I give to you. I have got an orc-blade, but I do not think it will be my part to strike any blow again.'

It was difficult and dangerous moving in the night in the pathless land; but slowly and with much stumbling the two hobbits toiled on hour by hour northward along the eastern edge of the stony valley. When a grey light crept back over the western heights, long after day had opened in the lands beyond, they went into hiding again and slept a little, turn by turn. In his times of waking Sam was busy with thoughts of food. At last when Frodo roused himself and spoke of eating and making ready for yet another effort, he asked the question that was troubling him most.

'Begging your pardon, Mr. Frodo,' he said, 'but have you any notion how far there is still to go?'

'No, not any clear notion, Sam,' Frodo answered. 'In Rivendell before I set out I was shown a map of Mordor that was made before the Enemy came back here; but I only remember it vaguely. I remember clearest that there was a place in the north where the western range and the northern range send out spurs that nearly meet. That must be twenty leagues at least from the bridge back by the Tower. It might be a good point at which to cross. But of course, if we get there, we shall be further than we were from the Mountain, sixty miles from it, I should think. I guess that we have gone about twelve leagues north from the bridge now. Even if all goes well, I could hardly reach the Mountain in a week. I am afraid, Sam, that the burden will get very heavy, and I shall go still slower as we get nearer.'

Sam sighed. 'That's just as I feared,' he said. 'Well, to say nothing of water, we've got to eat less, Mr. Frodo, or else move a bit quicker, at any rate while we're still in this valley. One more bite and all the food's ended, save the Elves' waybread.'

'I'll try and be a bit quicker, Sam,' said Frodo, drawing a deep breath. 'Come on then! Let's start another march!'

It was not yet quite dark again. They plodded along, on into the night. The hours passed in a weary stumbling trudge with a few brief halts. At the first hint of grey light under the skirts of the canopy of shadow they hid themselves again in a dark hollow under an overhanging stone.

Slowly the light grew, until it was clearer than it yet had been. A strong wind from the West was now driving the fumes of Mordor from the upper airs. Before long the hobbits could make out the shape of the land for some miles about them. The trough between the mountains and the Morgai had steadily dwindled as it climbed upwards, and the inner ridge was now no more than a shelf in the steep faces of the Ephel Dúath; but to the east it fell as sheerly as ever down into Gorgoroth. Ahead the water-course came to an end in broken steps of rock; for out from the main range there sprang a high barren spur, thrusting eastward like a wall. To meet it there stretched out from the grey and misty northern range of Ered Lithui a long jutting arm; and between the

ends there was a narrow gap: Carach Angren, the Isenmouthe, beyond which lay the deep dale of Udûn. In that
dale behind the Morannon were the tunnels and deep
armouries that the servants of Mordor had made for the
defence of the Black Gate of their land; and there now their
Lord was gathering in haste great forces to meet the onslaught
of the Captains of the West. Upon the out-thrust spurs forts
and towers were built, and watch-fires burned; and all across
the gap an earth-wall had been raised, and a deep trench
delved that could be crossed only by a single bridge.

A few miles north, high up in the angle where the western
spur branched away from the main range, stood the old castle
of Durthang, now one of the many orc-holds that clustered
about the dale of Udûn. A road, already visible in the growing
light, came winding down from it, until only a mile or two
from where the hobbits lay it turned east and ran along a
shelf cut in the side of the spur, and so went down into the
plain, and on to the Isenmouthe.

To the hobbits as they looked out it seemed that all their
journey north had been useless. The plain to their right was
dim and smoky, and they could see there neither camps nor
troops moving; but all that region was under the vigilance of
the forts of Carach Angren.

'We have come to a dead end, Sam,' said Frodo. 'If we
go on, we shall only come up to that orc-tower, but the only
road to take is that road that comes down from it – unless
we go back. We can't climb up westward, or climb down
eastward.'

'Then we must take the road, Mr. Frodo,' said Sam. 'We
must take it and chance our luck, if there is any luck in
Mordor. We might as well give ourselves up as wander about
any more, or try to go back. Our food won't last. We've got
to make a dash for it!'

'All right, Sam,' said Frodo. 'Lead me! As long as you've
got any hope left. Mine is gone. But I can't dash, Sam. I'll
just plod along after you.'

'Before you start any more plodding, you need sleep and

food, Mr. Frodo. Come and take what you can get of them!'

He gave Frodo water and an additional wafer of the way-bread, and he made a pillow of his cloak for his master's head. Frodo was too weary to debate the matter, and Sam did not tell him that he had drunk the last drop of their water, and eaten Sam's share of the food as well as his own. When Frodo was asleep Sam bent over him and listened to his breathing and scanned his face. It was lined and thin, and yet in sleep it looked content and unafraid. 'Well, here goes, Master!' Sam muttered to himself. 'I'll have to leave you for a bit and trust to luck. Water we must have, or we'll get no further.'

Sam crept out, and flitting from stone to stone with more than hobbit-care, he went down to the water-course, and then followed it for some way as it climbed north, until he came to the rock-steps where long ago, no doubt, its spring had come gushing down in a little waterfall. All now seemed dry and silent; but refusing to despair Sam stooped and listened, and to his delight he caught the sound of trickling. Clambering a few steps up he found a tiny stream of dark water that came out from the hill-side and filled a little bare pool, from which again it spilled, and vanished then under the barren stones.

Sam tasted the water, and it seemed good enough. Then he drank deeply, refilled the bottle, and turned to go back. At that moment he caught a glimpse of a black form or shadow flitting among the rocks away near Frodo's hiding-place. Biting back a cry, he leapt down from the spring and ran, jumping from stone to stone. It was a wary creature, difficult to see, but Sam had little doubt about it: he longed to get his hands on its neck. But it heard him coming and slipped quickly away. Sam thought he saw a last fleeting glimpse of it, peering back over the edge of the eastward precipice, before it ducked and disappeared.

'Well, luck did not let me down,' muttered Sam, 'but that was a near thing! Isn't it enough to have orcs by the thousand without that stinking villain coming nosing round? I wish he had been shot!' He sat down by Frodo and did not rouse him; but he did not dare to go to sleep himself. At last when he felt his eyes closing and knew that his struggle to keep awake could not go on much longer, he wakened Frodo gently.

'That Gollum's about again, I'm afraid, Mr. Frodo,' he said. 'Leastways, if it wasn't him, then there's two of him. I went away to find some water and spied him nosing round just as I turned back. I reckon it isn't safe for us both to sleep together, and begging your pardon, but I can't hold up my lids much longer.'

'Bless you, Sam!' said Frodo. 'Lie down and take your proper turn! But I'd rather have Gollum than orcs. At any rate he won't give us away to them – not unless he's caught himself.'

'But he might do a bit of robbery and murder on his own,' growled Sam. 'Keep your eyes open, Mr. Frodo! There's a bottle full of water. Drink up. We can fill it again when we go on.' With that Sam plunged into sleep.

Light was fading again when he woke. Frodo sat propped against the rock behind, but he had fallen asleep. The water-bottle was empty. There was no sign of Gollum.

Mordor-dark had returned, and the watch-fires on the heights burned fierce and red, when the hobbits set out again on the most dangerous stage of all their journey. They went first to the little spring, and then climbing warily up they came to the road at the point where it swung east towards the Isenmouthe twenty miles away. It was not a broad road, and it had no wall or parapet along the edge, and as it ran on the sheer drop from its brink became deeper and deeper. The hobbits could hear no movements, and after listening for a while they set off eastward at a steady pace.

After doing some twelve miles, they halted. A short way back the road had bent a little northward and the stretch that they had passed over was now screened from sight. This proved disastrous. They rested for some minutes and then went on; but they had not taken many steps when suddenly in the stillness of the night they heard the sound that all along they had secretly dreaded: the noise of marching feet. It was still some way behind them, but looking back they could see the twinkle of torches coming round the bend less than a mile away, and they were moving fast: too fast for Frodo to escape by flight along the road ahead.

'I feared it, Sam,' said Frodo. 'We've trusted to luck, and it has failed us. We're trapped.' He looked wildly up at the frowning wall, where the road-builders of old had cut the rock sheer for many fathoms above their heads. He ran to the other side and looked over the brink into a dark pit of gloom. 'We're trapped at last!' he said. He sank to the ground beneath the wall of rock and bowed his head.

'Seems so,' said Sam. 'Well, we can but wait and see.' And with that he sat down beside Frodo under the shadow of the cliff.

They did not have to wait long. The orcs were going at a great pace. Those in the foremost files bore torches. On they came, red flames in the dark, swiftly growing. Now Sam too bowed his head, hoping that it would hide his face when the torches reached them; and he set their shields before their knees to hide their feet.

'If only they are in a hurry and will let a couple of tired soldiers alone and pass on!' he thought.

And so it seemed that they would. The leading orcs came loping along, panting, holding their heads down. They were a gang of the smaller breeds being driven unwilling to their Dark Lord's wars; all they cared for was to get the march over and escape the whip. Beside them, running up and down the line, went two of the large fierce *uruks*, cracking lashes and shouting. File after file passed, and the tell-tale torchlight was already some way ahead. Sam held his breath. Now more than half the line had gone by. Then suddenly one of the slave-drivers spied the two figures by the road-side. He flicked a whip at them and yelled: 'Hi, you! Get up!' They did not answer, and with a shout he halted the whole company.

'Come on, you slugs!' he cried. 'This is no time for slouching.' He took a step towards them, and even in the gloom he recognized the devices on their shields. 'Deserting, eh?' he snarled. 'Or thinking of it? All your folk should have been inside Udûn before yesterday evening. You know that. Up you get and fall in, or I'll have your numbers and report you.'

They struggled to their feet, and keeping bent, limping like footsore soldiers, they shuffled back towards the rear of the line. 'No, not at the rear!' the slave-driver shouted. 'Three files up. And stay there, or you'll know it, when I come down the line!' He sent his long whip-lash cracking over their heads; then with another crack and a yell he started the company off again at a brisk trot.

It was hard enough for poor Sam, tired as he was; but for Frodo it was a torment, and soon a nightmare. He set his teeth and tried to stop his mind from thinking, and he struggled on. The stench of the sweating orcs about him was stifling, and he began to gasp with thirst. On, on they went, and he bent all his will to draw his breath and to make his legs keep going; and yet to what evil end he toiled and endured he did not dare to think. There was no hope of falling out unseen. Now and again the orc-driver fell back and jeered at them.

'There now!' he laughed, flicking at their legs. 'Where there's a whip there's a will, my slugs. Hold up! I'd give you a nice freshener now, only you'll get as much lash as your skins will carry when you come in late to your camp. Do you good. Don't you know we're at war?'

They had gone some miles, and the road was at last running down a long slope into the plain, when Frodo's strength began to give out and his will wavered. He lurched and stumbled. Desperately Sam tried to help him and hold him up, though he felt that he could himself hardly stay the pace much longer. At any moment now he knew that the end would come: his master would faint or fall, and all would be discovered, and their bitter efforts be in vain. 'I'll have that big slave-driving devil anyway,' he thought.

Then just as he was putting his hand to the hilt of his sword, there came an unexpected relief. They were out on the plain now and drawing near the entrance to Udûn. Some way in front of it, before the gate at the bridge-end, the road from the west converged with others coming from the south, and from Barad-dûr. Along all the roads troops were moving; for the Captains of the West were advancing and the Dark Lord was speeding his forces north. So it chanced that several companies came together at the road-meeting, in the dark beyond the light of the watch-fires on the wall. At once there was great jostling and cursing as each troop tried to get first to the gate and the ending of their march. Though the drivers yelled and plied their whips, scuffles broke out and some blades were drawn. A troop of heavy-armed *uruks* from Barad-dûr charged into the Durthang line and threw them into confusion.

Dazed as he was with pain and weariness, Sam woke up, grasped quickly at his chance, and threw himself to the ground, dragging Frodo down with him. Orcs fell over them, snarling and cursing. Slowly on hand and knee the hobbits crawled away out of the turmoil, until at last unnoticed they dropped over the further edge of the road. It had a high kerb by which troop-leaders could guide themselves in black night or fog, and it was banked up some feet above the level of the open land.

They lay still for a while. It was too dark to seek for cover, if indeed there was any to find; but Sam felt that they ought at least to get further away from the highways and out of the range of torchlight.

'Come on, Mr. Frodo!' he whispered. 'One more crawl, and then you can lie still.'

With a last despairing effort Frodo raised himself on his hands, and struggled on for maybe twenty yards. Then he pitched down into a shallow pit that opened unexpectedly before them, and there he lay like a dead thing.

CHAPTER III

MOUNT DOOM

Sam put his ragged orc-cloak under his master's head, and covered them both with the grey robe of Lórien; and as he did so his thoughts went out to that fair land, and to the Elves, and he hoped that the cloth woven by their hands might have some virtue to keep them hidden beyond all hope in this wilderness of fear. He heard the scuffling and cries die down as the troops passed on through the Isenmouthe. It seemed that in the confusion and the mingling of many companies of various kinds they had not been missed, not yet at any rate.

Sam took a sip of water, but pressed Frodo to drink, and when his master had recovered a little he gave him a whole wafer of their precious waybread and made him eat it. Then, too worn out even to feel much fear, they stretched themselves out. They slept a little in uneasy fits; for their sweat grew chill on them, and the hard stones bit them, and they shivered. Out of the north from the Black Gate through Cirith Gorgor there flowed whispering along the ground a thin cold air.

In the morning a grey light came again, for in the high regions the West Wind still blew, but down on the stones behind the fences of the Black Land the air seemed almost dead, chill and yet stifling. Sam looked up out of the hollow. The land all about was dreary, flat and drab-hued. On the roads nearby nothing was moving now; but Sam feared the watchful eyes on the wall of the Isenmouthe, no more than a furlong away northward. South-eastward, far off like a dark standing shadow, loomed the Mountain. Smokes were pouring from it, and while those that rose into the upper air trailed away eastward, great rolling clouds floated down its sides and spread over the land. A few miles to the north-east the foothills of the Ashen Mountains stood like sombre grey ghosts, behind which the misty northern heights rose like a line of distant cloud hardly darker than the lowering sky.

Sam tried to guess the distances and to decide what way they ought to take. 'It looks every step of fifty miles,' he muttered gloomily, staring at the threatening mountain, 'and that'll take a week, if it takes a day, with Mr. Frodo as he is.' He shook his head, and as he worked things out, slowly a new dark thought grew in his mind. Never for long had hope died in his staunch heart, and always until now he had taken some thought for their return. But the bitter truth came home to him at last: at best their provision would take them to their goal; and when the task was done, there they would come to an end, alone, houseless, foodless in the midst of a terrible desert. There could be no return.

'So that was the job I felt I had to do when I started,' thought Sam: 'to help Mr. Frodo to the last step and then die with him? Well, if that is the job then I must do it. But I would dearly like to see Bywater again, and Rosie Cotton and her brothers, and the Gaffer and Marigold and all. I can't think somehow that Gandalf would have sent Mr. Frodo on this errand, if there hadn't a' been any hope of his ever coming back at all. Things all went wrong when he went down in Moria. I wish he hadn't. He would have done something.'

But even as hope died in Sam, or seemed to die, it was turned to a new strength. Sam's plain hobbit-face grew stern, almost grim, as the will hardened in him, and he felt through all his limbs a thrill, as if he was turning into some creature of stone and steel that neither despair nor weariness nor endless barren miles could subdue.

With a new sense of responsibility he brought his eyes back to the ground near at hand, studying the next move. As the light grew a little he saw to his surprise that what from a distance had seemed wide and featureless flats were in fact all broken and tumbled. Indeed the whole surface of the plains of Gorgoroth was pocked with great holes, as if, while it was still a waste of soft mud, it had been smitten with a shower of bolts and huge slingstones. The largest of these holes were rimmed with ridges of broken rock, and broad fissures ran out from them in all directions. It was a land in which it would be possible to creep from hiding to hiding, unseen by all but the most watchful eyes: possible at least for one who was strong and had no need for speed. For the hungry and worn, who had far to go before life failed, it had an evil look.

Thinking of all these things Sam went back to his master. He had no need to rouse him. Frodo was lying on his back with eyes open, staring at the cloudy sky. 'Well, Mr. Frodo,' said Sam, 'I've been having a look round and thinking a bit. There's nothing on the roads, and we'd best be getting away while there's a chance. Can you manage it?'

'I can manage it,' said Frodo. 'I must.'

Once more they started, crawling from hollow to hollow, flitting behind such cover as they could find, but moving always in a slant towards the foothills of the northern range. But as they went the most easterly of the roads followed them, until it ran off, hugging the skirts of the mountains, away into a wall of black shadow far ahead. Neither man nor orc now moved along its flat grey stretches; for the Dark Lord had almost completed the movement of his forces, and even in the fastness of his own realm he sought the secrecy of night, fearing the winds of the world that had turned against him, tearing aside his veils, and troubled with tidings of bold spies that had passed through his fences.

The hobbits had gone a few weary miles when they halted. Frodo seemed nearly spent. Sam saw that he could not go much further in this fashion, crawling, stooping, now picking a doubtful way very slowly, now hurrying at a stumbling run.

'I'm going back on to the road while the light lasts, Mr. Frodo,' he said. 'Trust to luck again! It nearly failed us last time, but it didn't quite. A steady pace for a few more miles, and then a rest.'

He was taking a far greater risk than he knew; but Frodo was too much occupied with his burden and with the struggle in his mind to debate, and almost too hopeless to care. They climbed on to the causeway and trudged along, down the hard cruel road that led to the Dark Tower itself. But their luck held, and for the rest of that day they met no living or moving thing; and when night fell they vanished into the darkness of Mordor. All the land now brooded as at the coming of a great storm: for the Captains of the West had passed the Cross-roads and set flames in the deadly fields of Imlad Morgul.

So the desperate journey went on, as the Ring went south and the banners of the kings rode north. For the hobbits each day, each mile, was more bitter than the one before, as their strength lessened and the land became more evil. They met no enemies by day. At times by night, as they cowered or drowsed uneasily in some hiding beside the road, they heard cries and the noise of many feet or the swift passing of some cruelly ridden steed. But far worse than all such perils was the ever-approaching threat that beat upon them as they went: the dreadful menace of the Power that waited, brooding in deep thought and sleepless malice behind the dark veil about its Throne. Nearer and nearer it drew, looming blacker, like the oncoming of a wall of night at the last end of the world.

There came at last a dreadful nightfall; and even as the Captains of the West drew near to the end of the living lands, the two wanderers came to an hour of blank despair. Four days had passed since they had escaped from the orcs, but the time lay behind them like an ever-darkening dream. All this last day Frodo had not spoken, but had walked half-bowed, often stumbling, as if his eyes no longer saw the way before his feet. Sam guessed that among all their pains he bore the worst, the growing weight of the Ring, a burden on the body and a torment to his mind. Anxiously Sam had noted how his master's left hand would often be raised as if to ward off a blow, or to screen his shrinking eyes from a dreadful Eye that sought to look in them. And sometimes his right hand would creep to his breast, clutching, and then slowly, as the will recovered mastery, it would be withdrawn.

Now as the blackness of night returned Frodo sat, his head between his knees, his arms hanging wearily to the ground where his hands lay feebly twitching. Sam watched him, till night covered them both and hid them from one another. He could no longer find any words to say; and he turned to his own dark thoughts. As for himself, though weary and under a shadow of fear, he still had some strength left. The *lembas* had a virtue without which they would long ago have lain down to die. It did not satisfy desire, and at times Sam's mind was filled with the memories of food, and the longing for simple bread and meats. And yet this waybread of the Elves had a potency that increased as travellers relied on it alone and did not mingle it with other foods. It fed the will, and it gave strength to endure, and to master sinew and limb beyond the measure of mortal kind. But now a new decision must be made. They could not follow this road any longer; for it went on eastward into the great Shadow, but the Mountain now loomed upon their right, almost due south, and they must turn towards it. Yet still before it there stretched a wide region of fuming, barren, ash-ridden land.

'Water, water!' muttered Sam. He had stinted himself, and in his parched mouth his tongue seemed thick and swollen; but for all his care they now had very little left, perhaps half his bottle, and maybe there were still days to go. All would long ago have been spent, if they had not dared to follow the orc-road. For at long intervals on that highway cisterns had been built for the use of troops sent in haste through the waterless regions. In one Sam had found some water left, stale, muddied by the orcs, but still sufficient for their desperate case. Yet that was now a day ago. There was no hope of any more.

At last wearied with his cares Sam drowsed, leaving the

morrow till it came; he could do no more. Dream and waking
mingled uneasily. He saw lights like gloating eyes, and dark
creeping shapes, and he heard noises as of wild beasts or the
dreadful cries of tortured things; and he would start up to
find the world all dark and only empty blackness all about
him. Once only, as he stood and stared wildly round, did it
seem that, though now awake, he could still see pale lights
like eyes; but soon they flickered and vanished.

The hateful night passed slowly and reluctantly. Such daylight as followed was dim; for here as the Mountain drew
near the air was ever mirky, while out from the Dark Tower
there crept the veils of Shadow that Sauron wove about himself. Frodo was lying on his back not moving. Sam stood
beside him, reluctant to speak, and yet knowing that the word
now lay with him: he must set his master's will to work
for another effort. At length, stooping and caressing Frodo's
brow, he spoke in his ear.

'Wake up, Master!' he said. 'Time for another start.'

As if roused by a sudden bell, Frodo rose quickly, and
stood up and looked away southwards; but when his eyes
beheld the Mountain and the desert he quailed again.

'I can't manage it, Sam,' he said. 'It is such a weight to
carry, such a weight.'

Sam knew before he spoke, that it was vain, and that such
words might do more harm than good, but in his pity he
could not keep silent. 'Then let me carry it a bit for you,
Master,' he said. 'You know I would, and gladly, as long as
I have any strength.'

A wild light came into Frodo's eyes. 'Stand away! Don't
touch me!' he cried. 'It is mine, I say. Be off!' His hand
strayed to his sword-hilt. But then quickly his voice changed.
'No, no, Sam,' he said sadly. 'But you must understand. It
is my burden, and no one else can bear it. It is too late now,
Sam dear. You can't help me in that way again. I am almost
in its power now. I could not give it up, and if you tried to
take it I should go mad.'

Sam nodded. 'I understand,' he said. 'But I've been thinking, Mr. Frodo, there's other things we might do without.
Why not lighten the load a bit? We're going that way now,
as straight as we can make it.' He pointed to the Mountain.
'It's no good taking anything we're not sure to need.'

Frodo looked again towards the Mountain. 'No,' he said,
'we shan't need much on that road. And at its end nothing.'
Picking up his orc-shield he flung it away and threw his
helmet after it. Then pulling off the grey cloak he undid the
heavy belt and let it fall to the ground, and the sheathed
sword with it. The shreds of the black cloak he tore off and
scattered.

'There, I'll be an orc no more,' he cried, 'and I'll bear no
weapon, fair or foul. Let them take me, if they will!'

Sam did likewise, and put aside his orc-gear; and he took
out all the things in his pack. Somehow each of them had
become dear to him, if only because he had borne them so
far with so much toil. Hardest of all it was to part with his
cooking-gear. Tears welled in his eyes at the thought of cast-
ing it away.

'Do you remember that bit of rabbit, Mr. Frodo?' he said.
'And our place under the warm bank in Captain Faramir's
country, the day I saw an oliphaunt?'

'No, I am afraid not, Sam,' said Frodo. 'At least, I know
that such things happened, but I cannot see them. No taste
of food, no feel of water, no sound of wind, no memory of
tree or grass or flower, no image of moon or star are left to
me. I am naked in the dark, Sam, and there is no veil between
me and the wheel of fire. I begin to see it even with my
waking eyes, and all else fades.'

Sam went to him and kissed his hand. 'Then the sooner
we're rid of it, the sooner to rest,' he said haltingly, finding
no better words to say. 'Talking won't mend nothing,' he
muttered to himself, as he gathered up all the things that
they had chosen to cast away. He was not willing to leave
them lying open in the wilderness for any eyes to see. 'Stinker
picked up that orc-shirt, seemingly, and he isn't going to add

a sword to it. His hands are bad enough when empty. And he isn't going to mess with my pans!' With that he carried all the gear away to one of the many gaping fissures that scored the land and threw them in. The clatter of his precious pans as they fell down into the dark was like a death-knell to his heart.

He came back to Frodo, and then of his elven-rope he cut a short piece to serve his master as a girdle and bind the grey cloak close about his waist. The rest he carefully coiled and put back in his pack. Beside that he kept only the remnants of their waybread and the water-bottle, and Sting still hanging by his belt; and hidden away in a pocket of his tunic next his breast the phial of Galadriel and the little box that she gave him for his own.

Now at last they turned their faces to the Mountain and set out, thinking no more of concealment, bending their weariness and failing wills only to the one task of going on. In the dimness of its dreary day few things even in that land of vigilance could have espied them, save from close at hand. Of all the slaves of the Dark Lord, only the Nazgûl could have warned him of the peril that crept, small but indomitable, into the very heart of his guarded realm. But the Nazgûl and their black wings were abroad on other errand: they were gathered far away, shadowing the march of the Captains of the West, and thither the thought of the Dark Tower was turned.

That day it seemed to Sam that his master had found some new strength, more than could be explained by the small lightening of the load that he had to carry. In the first marches they went further and faster than he had hoped. The land was rough and hostile, and yet they made much progress, and ever the Mountain drew nearer. But as the day wore on and all too soon the dim light began to fail, Frodo stooped again, and began to stagger, as if the renewed effort had squandered his remaining strength.

At their last halt he sank down and said: 'I'm thirsty, Sam,' and did not speak again. Sam gave him a mouthful of water;

only one more mouthful remained. He went without himself;
and now as once more the night of Mordor closed over them,
through all his thoughts there came the memory of water;
and every brook or stream or fount that he had ever seen,
under green willow-shades or twinkling in the sun, danced
and rippled for his torment behind the blindness of his eyes.
He felt the cool mud about his toes as he paddled in the Pool
at Bywater with Jolly Cotton and Tom and Nibs, and their
sister Rosie. 'But that was years ago,' he sighed, 'and far
away. The way back, if there is one, goes past the Mountain.'

He could not sleep and he held a debate with himself.
'Well, come now, we've done better than you hoped,' he said
sturdily. 'Began well anyway. I reckon we crossed half the
distance before we stopped. One more day will do it.' And
then he paused.

'Don't be a fool, Sam Gamgee,' came an answer in his
own voice. 'He won't go another day like that, if he moves
at all. And you can't go on much longer giving him all the
water and most of the food.'

'I can go on a good way though, and I will.'

'Where to?'

'To the Mountain, of course.'

'But what then, Sam Gamgee, what then? When you get
there, what are you going to do? He won't be able to do
anything for himself.'

To his dismay Sam realized that he had not got an answer
to this. He had no clear idea at all. Frodo had not spoken
much to him of his errand, and Sam only knew vaguely that
the Ring had somehow to be put into the fire. 'The Cracks
of Doom,' he muttered, the old name rising to his mind.
'Well, if Master knows how to find them, I don't.'

'There you are!' came the answer. 'It's all quite useless.
He said so himself. You are the fool, going on hoping and
toiling. You could have lain down and gone to sleep together
days ago, if you hadn't been so dogged. But you'll die just
the same, or worse. You might just as well lie down now and
give it up. You'll never get to the top anyway.'

'I'll get there, if I leave everything but my bones behind,' said Sam. 'And I'll carry Mr. Frodo up myself, if it breaks my back and heart. So stop arguing!'

At that moment Sam felt a tremor in the ground beneath him, and he heard or sensed a deep remote rumble as of thunder imprisoned under the earth. There was a brief red flame that flickered under the clouds and died away. The Mountain too slept uneasily.

The last stage of their journey to Orodruin came, and it was a torment greater than Sam had ever thought that he could bear. He was in pain, and so parched that he could no longer swallow even a mouthful of food. It remained dark, not only because of the smokes of the Mountain: there seemed to be a storm coming up, and away to the south-east there was a shimmer of lightnings under the black skies. Worst of all, the air was full of fumes; breathing was painful and difficult, and a dizziness came on them, so that they staggered and often fell. And yet their wills did not yield, and they struggled on.

The Mountain crept up ever nearer, until, if they lifted their heavy heads, it filled all their sight, looming vast before them: a huge mass of ash and slag and burned stone, out of which a sheer-sided cone was raised into the clouds. Before the daylong dusk ended and true night came again they had crawled and stumbled to its very feet.

With a gasp Frodo cast himself on the ground. Sam sat by him. To his surprise he felt tired but lighter, and his head seemed clear again. No more debates disturbed his mind. He knew all the arguments of despair and would not listen to them. His will was set, and only death would break it. He felt no longer either desire or need of sleep, but rather of watchfulness. He knew that all the hazards and perils were now drawing together to a point: the next day would be a day of doom, the day of final effort or disaster, the last gasp.

But when would it come? The night seemed endless and timeless, minute after minute falling dead and adding up to

no passing hour, bringing no change. Sam began to wonder
if a second darkness had begun and no day would ever
reappear. At last he groped for Frodo's hand. It was cold
and trembling. His master was shivering.

'I didn't ought to have left my blanket behind,' muttered
Sam; and lying down he tried to comfort Frodo with his arms
and body. Then sleep took him, and the dim light of the last
day of their quest found them side by side. The wind had
fallen the day before as it shifted from the West, and now it
came from the North and began to rise; and slowly the light
of the unseen Sun filtered down into the shadows where the
hobbits lay.

'Now for it! Now for the last gasp!' said Sam as he struggled
to his feet. He bent over Frodo, rousing him gently. Frodo
groaned; but with a great effort of will he staggered up; and
then he fell upon his knees again. He raised his eyes with
difficulty to the dark slopes of Mount Doom towering above
him, and then pitifully he began to crawl forward on his
hands.

Sam looked at him and wept in his heart, but no tears
came to his dry and stinging eyes. 'I said I'd carry him, if it
broke my back,' he muttered, 'and I will!'

'Come, Mr. Frodo!' he cried. 'I can't carry it for you, but
I can carry you and it as well. So up you get! Come on, Mr.
Frodo dear! Sam will give you a ride. Just tell him where to
go, and he'll go.'

As Frodo clung upon his back, arms loosely about his neck,
legs clasped firmly under his arms, Sam staggered to his feet;
and then to his amazement he felt the burden light. He had
feared that he would have barely strength to lift his master
alone, and beyond that he had expected to share in the dreadful dragging weight of the accursed Ring. But it was not so.
Whether because Frodo was so worn by his long pains,
wound of knife, and venomous sting, and sorrow, fear, and
homeless wandering, or because some gift of final strength
was given to him, Sam lifted Frodo with no more difficulty

than if he were carrying a hobbit-child pig-a-back in some romp on the lawns or hayfields of the Shire. He took a deep breath and started off.

They had reached the Mountain's foot on its northern side, and a little to the westward; there its long grey slopes, though broken, were not sheer. Frodo did not speak, and so Sam struggled on as best he could, having no guidance but the will to climb as high as might be before his strength gave out and his will broke. On he toiled, up and up, turning this way and that to lessen the slope, often stumbling forward, and at the last crawling like a snail with a heavy burden on its back. When his will could drive him no further, and his limbs gave way, he stopped and laid his master gently down.

Frodo opened his eyes and drew a breath. It was easier to breathe up here above the reeks that coiled and drifted down below. 'Thank you, Sam,' he said in a cracked whisper. 'How far is there to go?'

'I don't know,' said Sam, 'because I don't know where we're going.'

He looked back, and then he looked up; and he was amazed to see how far his last effort had brought him. The Mountain standing ominous and alone had looked taller than it was. Sam saw now that it was less lofty than the high passes of the Ephel Dúath which he and Frodo had scaled. The confused and tumbled shoulders of its great base rose for maybe three thousand feet above the plain, and above them was reared half as high again its tall central cone, like a vast oast or chimney capped with a jagged crater. But already Sam was more than half way up the base, and the plain of Gorgoroth was dim below him, wrapped in fume and shadow. As he looked up he would have given a shout, if his parched throat had allowed him; for amid the rugged humps and shoulders above him he saw plainly a path or road. It climbed like a rising girdle from the west and wound snakelike about the Mountain, until before it went round out of view it reached the foot of the cone upon its eastern side.

Sam could not see the course immediately above him, where it was lowest, for a steep slope went up from where he stood; but he guessed that if he could only struggle on just a little way further up, they would strike this path. A gleam of hope returned to him. They might conquer the Mountain yet. 'Why, it might have been put there a-purpose!' he said to himself. 'If it wasn't there, I'd have to say I was beaten in the end.'

The path was not put there for the purposes of Sam. He did not know it, but he was looking at Sauron's Road from Barad-dûr to the Sammath Naur, the Chambers of Fire. Out from the Dark Tower's huge western gate it came over a deep abyss by a vast bridge of iron, and then passing into the plain it ran for a league between two smoking chasms, and so reached a long sloping causeway that led up on to the Mountain's eastern side. Thence, turning and encircling all its wide girth from south to north, it climbed at last, high in the upper cone, but still far from the reeking summit, to a dark entrance that gazed back east straight to the Window of the Eye in Sauron's shadow-mantled fortress. Often blocked or destroyed by the tumults of the Mountain's furnaces, always that road was repaired and cleared again by the labours of countless orcs.

Sam drew a deep breath. There was a path, but how he was to get up the slope to it he did not know. First he must ease his aching back. He lay flat beside Frodo for a while. Neither spoke. Slowly the light grew. Suddenly a sense of urgency which he did not understand came to Sam. It was almost as if he had been called: 'Now, now, or it will be too late!' He braced himself and got up. Frodo also seemed to have felt the call. He struggled to his knees.

'I'll crawl, Sam,' he gasped.

So foot by foot, like small grey insects, they crept up the slope. They came to the path and found that it was broad, paved with broken rubble and beaten ash. Frodo clambered on to it, and then moved as if by some compulsion he turned slowly to face the East. Far off the shadows of Sauron hung;

but torn by some gust of wind out of the world, or else moved by some great disquiet within, the mantling clouds swirled, and for a moment drew aside; and then he saw, rising black, blacker and darker than the vast shades amid which it stood, the cruel pinnacles and iron crown of the topmost tower of Barad-dûr. One moment only it stared out, but as from some great window immeasurably high there stabbed northward a flame of red, the flicker of a piercing Eye; and then the shadows were furled again and the terrible vision was removed. The Eye was not turned to them: it was gazing north to where the Captains of the West stood at bay, and thither all its malice was now bent, as the Power moved to strike its deadly blow; but Frodo at that dreadful glimpse fell as one stricken mortally. His hand sought the chain about his neck.

Sam knelt by him. Faint, almost inaudibly, he heard Frodo whispering: 'Help me, Sam! Help me, Sam! Hold my hand! I can't stop it.' Sam took his master's hands and laid them together, palm to palm, and kissed them; and then he held them gently between his own. The thought came suddenly to him: 'He's spotted us! It's all up, or it soon will be. Now, Sam Gamgee, this is the end of ends.'

Again he lifted Frodo and drew his hands down to his own breast, letting his master's legs dangle. Then he bowed his head and struggled off along the climbing road. It was not as easy a way to take as it had looked at first. By fortune the fires that had poured forth in the great turmoils when Sam stood upon Cirith Ungol had flowed down mainly on the southern and western slopes, and the road on this side was not blocked. Yet in many places it had crumbled away or was crossed by gaping rents. After climbing eastward for some time it bent back upon itself at a sharp angle and went westward for a space. There at the bend it was cut deep through a crag of old weathered stone once long ago vomited from the Mountain's furnaces. Panting under his load Sam turned the bend; and even as he did so, out of the corner of his eye, he had a glimpse of something falling from the crag, like a small piece of black stone that had toppled off as he passed.

A sudden weight smote him and he crashed forward, tearing the backs of his hands that still clasped his master's. Then he knew what had happened, for above him as he lay he heard a hated voice.

'Wicked masster!' it hissed. 'Wicked masster cheats us; cheats Sméagol, *gollum*. He musstn't go that way. He musstn't hurt Preciouss. Give it to Sméagol, yess, give it to us! Give it to uss!'

With a violent heave Sam rose up. At once he drew his sword; but he could do nothing. Gollum and Frodo were locked together. Gollum was tearing at his master, trying to get at the chain and the Ring. This was probably the only thing that could have roused the dying embers of Frodo's heart and will: an attack, an attempt to wrest his treasure from him by force. He fought back with a sudden fury that amazed Sam, and Gollum also. Even so things might have gone far otherwise, if Gollum himself had remained unchanged; but whatever dreadful paths, lonely and hungry and waterless, he had trodden, driven by a devouring desire and a terrible fear, they had left grievous marks on him. He was a lean, starved, haggard thing, all bones and tight-drawn sallow skin. A wild light flamed in his eyes, but his malice was no longer matched by his old griping strength. Frodo flung him off and rose up quivering.

'Down, down!' he gasped, clutching his hand to his breast, so that beneath the cover of his leather shirt he clasped the Ring. 'Down, you creeping thing, and out of my path! Your time is at an end. You cannot betray me or slay me now.'

Then suddenly, as before under the eaves of the Emyn Muil, Sam saw these two rivals with other vision. A crouching shape, scarcely more than the shadow of a living thing, a creature now wholly ruined and defeated, yet filled with a hideous lust and rage; and before it stood stern, untouchable now by pity, a figure robed in white, but at its breast it held a wheel of fire. Out of the fire there spoke a commanding voice.

'Begone, and trouble me no more! If you touch me ever again, you shall be cast yourself into the Fire of Doom.'

The crouching shape backed away, terror in its blinking eyes, and yet at the same time insatiable desire.

Then the vision passed and Sam saw Frodo standing, hand on breast, his breath coming in great gasps, and Gollum at his feet, resting on his knees with his wide-splayed hands upon the ground.

'Look out!' cried Sam. 'He'll spring!' He stepped forward, brandishing his sword. 'Quick, Master!' he gasped. 'Go on! Go on! No time to lose. I'll deal with him. Go on!'

Frodo looked at him as if at one now far away. 'Yes, I must go on,' he said. 'Farewell, Sam! This is the end at last. On Mount Doom doom shall fall. Farewell!' He turned and went on, walking slowly but erect, up the climbing path.

'Now!' said Sam. 'At last I can deal with you!' He leaped forward with drawn blade ready for battle. But Gollum did not spring. He fell flat upon the ground and whimpered.

'Don't kill us,' he wept. 'Don't hurt us with nassty cruel steel! Let us live, yes, live just a little longer. Lost lost! We're lost. And when Precious goes we'll die, yes, die into the dust.' He clawed up the ashes of the path with his long fleshless fingers. 'Dusst!' he hissed.

Sam's hand wavered. His mind was hot with wrath and the memory of evil. It would be just to slay this treacherous, murderous creature, just and many times deserved; and also it seemed the only safe thing to do. But deep in his heart there was something that restrained him: he could not strike this thing lying in the dust, forlorn, ruinous, utterly wretched. He himself, though only for a little while, had borne the Ring, and now dimly he guessed the agony of Gollum's shrivelled mind and body, enslaved to that Ring, unable to find peace or relief ever in life again. But Sam had no words to express what he felt.

'Oh, curse you, you stinking thing!' he said. 'Go away! Be off! I don't trust you, not as far as I could kick you; but be off. Or I *shall* hurt you, yes, with nasty cruel steel.'

Gollum got up on all fours, and backed away for several paces, and then he turned, and as Sam aimed a kick at him he fled away down the path. Sam gave no more heed to him. He suddenly remembered his master. He looked up the path and could not see him. As fast as he could he trudged up the road. If he had looked back, he might have seen not far below Gollum turn again, and then with a wild light of madness glaring in his eyes come, swiftly but warily, creeping on behind, a slinking shadow among the stones.

The path climbed on. Soon it bent again and with a last eastward course passed in a cutting along the face of the cone and came to the dark door in the Mountain's side, the door of the Sammath Naur. Far away now rising towards the South the sun, piercing the smokes and haze, burned ominous, a dull bleared disc of red; but all Mordor lay about the Mountain like a dead land, silent, shadow-folded, waiting for some dreadful stroke.

Sam came to the gaping mouth and peered in. It was dark and hot, and a deep rumbling shook the air. 'Frodo! Master!' he called. There was no answer. For a moment he stood, his heart beating with wild fears, and then he plunged in. A shadow followed him.

At first he could see nothing. In his great need he drew out once more the phial of Galadriel, but it was pale and cold in his trembling hand and threw no light into that stifling dark. He was come to the heart of the realm of Sauron and the forges of his ancient might, greatest in Middle-earth; all other powers were here subdued. Fearfully he took a few uncertain steps in the dark, and then all at once there came a flash of red that leaped upward, and smote the high black roof. Then Sam saw that he was in a long cave or tunnel that bored into the Mountain's smoking cone. But only a short way ahead its floor and the walls on either side were cloven by a great fissure, out of which the red glare came, now leaping up, now dying down into darkness; and all the while far below there was a rumour and a trouble as of great engines throbbing and labouring.

The light sprang up again, and there on the brink of the chasm, at the very Crack of Doom, stood Frodo, black against the glare, tense, erect, but still as if he had been turned to stone.

'Master!' cried Sam.

Then Frodo stirred and spoke with a clear voice, indeed with a voice clearer and more powerful than Sam had ever heard him use, and it rose above the throb and turmoil of Mount Doom, ringing in the roof and walls.

'I have come,' he said. 'But I do not choose now to do what I came to do. I will not do this deed. The Ring is mine!' And suddenly, as he set it on his finger, he vanished from Sam's sight. Sam gasped, but he had no chance to cry out, for at that moment many things happened.

Something struck Sam violently in the back, his legs were knocked from under him and he was flung aside, striking his head against the stony floor, as a dark shape sprang over him. He lay still and for a moment all went black.

And far away, as Frodo put on the Ring and claimed it for his own, even in Sammath Naur the very heart of his realm, the Power in Barad-dûr was shaken, and the Tower trembled from its foundations to its proud and bitter crown. The Dark Lord was suddenly aware of him, and his Eye piercing all shadows looked across the plain to the door that he had made; and the magnitude of his own folly was revealed to him in a blinding flash, and all the devices of his enemies were at last laid bare. Then his wrath blazed in consuming flame, but his fear rose like a vast black smoke to choke him. For he knew his deadly peril and the thread upon which his doom now hung.

From all his policies and webs of fear and treachery, from all his stratagems and wars his mind shook free; and throughout his realm a tremor ran, his slaves quailed, and his armies halted, and his captains suddenly steerless, bereft of will, wavered and despaired. For they were forgotten. The whole mind and purpose of the Power that wielded them was now bent with overwhelming force upon the Mountain. At his summons, wheeling with a rending cry, in a last desperate race there flew, faster than the winds, the Nazgûl, the Ring-wraiths, and with a storm of wings they hurtled southwards to Mount Doom.

Sam got up. He was dazed, and blood streaming from his head dripped in his eyes. He groped forward, and then he saw a strange and terrible thing. Gollum on the edge of the abyss was fighting like a mad thing with an unseen foe. To and fro he swayed, now so near the brink that almost he tumbled in, now dragging back, falling to the ground, rising, and falling again. And all the while he hissed but spoke no words.

The fires below awoke in anger, the red light blazed, and all the cavern was filled with a great glare and heat. Suddenly Sam saw Gollum's long hands draw upwards to his mouth; his white fangs gleamed, and then snapped as they bit. Frodo gave a cry, and there he was, fallen upon his knees at the chasm's edge. But Gollum, dancing like a mad thing, held aloft the ring, a finger still thrust within its circle. It shone now as if verily it was wrought of living fire.

'Precious, precious, precious!' Gollum cried. 'My Precious! O my Precious!' And with that, even as his eyes were lifted up to gloat on his prize, he stepped too far, toppled, wavered for a moment on the brink, and then with a shriek he fell. Out of the depths came his last wail *Precious*, and he was gone.

There was a roar and a great confusion of noise. Fires leaped up and licked the roof. The throbbing grew to a great tumult, and the Mountain shook. Sam ran to Frodo and picked him up and carried him out to the door. And there upon the dark threshold of the Sammath Naur, high above the plains of Mordor, such wonder and terror came on him that he stood still forgetting all else, and gazed as one turned to stone.

A brief vision he had of swirling cloud, and in the midst of it towers and battlements, tall as hills, founded upon a mighty mountain-throne above immeasurable pits; great courts and dungeons, eyeless prisons sheer as cliffs, and gaping gates of steel and adamant: and then all passed. Towers fell and mountains slid; walls crumbled and melted, crashing down; vast spires of smoke and spouting steams went billowing up, up, until they toppled like an overwhelming wave, and its wild crest curled and came foaming down upon the land. And then at last over the miles between there came a rumble, rising to a deafening crash and roar; the earth shook, the plain heaved and cracked, and Orodruin reeled. Fire belched from its riven summit. The skies burst into thunder seared with lightning. Down like lashing whips fell a torrent of black rain. And into the heart of the storm, with a cry that pierced all other sounds, tearing the clouds asunder, the Nazgûl came, shooting like flaming bolts, as caught in the fiery ruin of hill and sky they crackled, withered, and went out.

'Well, this is the end, Sam Gamgee,' said a voice by his side. And there was Frodo, pale and worn, and yet himself again; and in his eyes there was peace now, neither strain of will, nor madness, nor any fear. His burden was taken away. There was the dear master of the sweet days in the Shire.

'Master!' cried Sam, and fell upon his knees. In all that ruin of the world for the moment he felt only joy, great joy. The burden was gone. His master had been saved; he was himself again, he was free. And then Sam caught sight of the maimed and bleeding hand.

'Your poor hand!' he said. 'And I have nothing to bind it with, or comfort it. I would have spared him a whole hand of mine rather. But he's gone now beyond recall, gone for ever.'

'Yes,' said Frodo. 'But do you remember Gandalf's words:

Even Gollum may have something yet to do? But for him, Sam, I could not have destroyed the Ring. The Quest would have been in vain, even at the bitter end. So let us forgive him! For the Quest is achieved, and now all is over. I am glad you are here with me. Here at the end of all things, Sam.'

CHAPTER IV

THE FIELD OF CORMALLEN

All about the hills the hosts of Mordor raged. The Captains of the West were foundering in a gathering sea. The sun gleamed red, and under the wings of the Nazgûl the shadows of death fell dark upon the earth. Aragorn stood beneath his banner, silent and stern, as one lost in thought of things long past or far away; but his eyes gleamed like stars that shine the brighter as the night deepens. Upon the hill-top stood Gandalf, and he was white and cold and no shadow fell on him. The onslaught of Mordor broke like a wave on the beleaguered hills, voices roaring like a tide amid the wreck and crash of arms.

As if to his eyes some sudden vision had been given, Gandalf stirred; and he turned, looking back north where the skies were pale and clear. Then he lifted up his hands and cried in a loud voice ringing above the din: *The Eagles are coming!* And many voices answered crying: *The Eagles are coming! The Eagles are coming!* The hosts of Mordor looked up and wondered what this sign might mean.

There came Gwaihir the Windlord, and Landroval his brother, greatest of all the Eagles of the North, mightiest of the descendants of old Thorondor, who built his eyries in the inaccessible peaks of the Encircling Mountains when Middle-earth was young. Behind them in long swift lines came all their vassals from the northern mountains, speeding on a gathering wind. Straight down upon the Nazgûl they bore, stooping suddenly out of the high airs, and the rush of their wide wings as they passed over was like a gale.

But the Nazgûl turned and fled, and vanished into Mordor's shadows, hearing a sudden terrible call out of the Dark Tower; and even at that moment all the hosts of Mordor trembled, doubt clutched their hearts, their laughter failed, their hands shook and their limbs were loosed. The Power that drove them on and filled them with hate and fury was wavering, its will was removed from them; and now looking in the eyes of their enemies they saw a deadly light and were afraid.

Then all the Captains of the West cried aloud, for their hearts were filled with a new hope in the midst of darkness. Out from the beleaguered hills knights of Gondor, Riders of Rohan, Dúnedain of the North, close-serried companies, drove against their wavering foes, piercing the press with the thrust of bitter spears. But Gandalf lifted up his arms and called once more in a clear voice:

'Stand, Men of the West! Stand and wait! This is the hour of doom.'

And even as he spoke the earth rocked beneath their feet. Then rising swiftly up, far above the Towers of the Black Gate, high above the mountains, a vast soaring darkness sprang into the sky, flickering with fire. The earth groaned and quaked. The Towers of the Teeth swayed, tottered, and fell down; the mighty rampart crumbled; the Black Gate was hurled in ruin; and from far away, now dim, now growing, now mounting to the clouds, there came a drumming rumble, a roar, a long echoing roll of ruinous noise.

'The realm of Sauron is ended!' said Gandalf. 'The Ring-bearer has fulfilled his Quest.' And as the Captains gazed south to the Land of Mordor, it seemed to them that, black against the pall of cloud, there rose a huge shape of shadow, impenetrable, lightning-crowned, filling all the sky. Enormous it reared above the world, and stretched out towards them a vast threatening hand, terrible but impotent: for even as it leaned over them, a great wind took it, and it was all blown away, and passed; and then a hush fell.

The Captains bowed their heads; and when they looked up again, behold! their enemies were flying and the power of Mordor was scattering like dust in the wind. As when death smites the swollen brooding thing that inhabits their crawling hill and holds them all in sway, ants will wander witless and purposeless and then feebly die, so the creatures of Sauron, orc or troll or beast spell-enslaved, ran hither and thither mindless; and some slew themselves, or cast themselves in pits, or fled wailing back to hide in holes and dark lightless places far from hope. But the Men of Rhûn and of Harad, Easterling and Southron, saw the ruin of their war and the great majesty and glory of the Captains of the West. And those that were deepest and longest in evil servitude, hating the West, and yet were men proud and bold, in their turn now gathered themselves for a last stand of desperate battle. But the most part fled eastward as they could; and some cast their weapons down and sued for mercy.

Then Gandalf, leaving all such matters of battle and command to Aragorn and the other lords, stood upon the hill-top and called; and down to him came the great eagle, Gwaihir the Windlord, and stood before him.

'Twice you have borne me, Gwaihir my friend,' said Gandalf. 'Thrice shall pay for all, if you are willing. You will not find me a burden much greater than when you bore me from Zirakzigil, where my old life burned away.'

'I would bear you,' answered Gwaihir, 'whither you will, even were you made of stone.'

'Then come, and let your brother go with us, and some other of your folk who is most swift! For we have need of speed greater than any wind, outmatching the wings of the Nazgûl.'

'The North Wind blows, but we shall outfly it,' said Gwaihir. And he lifted up Gandalf and sped away south, and with him went Landroval, and Meneldor young and swift. And they passed over Udûn and Gorgoroth and saw all the land in ruin and tumult beneath them, and before them Mount Doom blazing, pouring out its fire.

*   *   *

'I am glad that you are here with me,' said Frodo. 'Here at the end of all things, Sam.'

'Yes, I am with you, Master,' said Sam, laying Frodo's wounded hand gently to his breast. 'And you're with me. And the journey's finished. But after coming all that way I don't want to give up yet. It's not like me, somehow, if you understand.'

'Maybe not, Sam,' said Frodo; 'but it's like things are in the world. Hopes fail. An end comes. We have only a little time to wait now. We are lost in ruin and downfall, and there is no escape.'

'Well, Master, we could at least go further from this dangerous place here, from this Crack of Doom, if that's its name. Now couldn't we? Come, Mr. Frodo, let's go down the path at any rate!'

'Very well, Sam. If you wish to go, I'll come,' said Frodo; and they rose and went slowly down the winding road; and even as they passed towards the Mountain's quaking feet, a great smoke and steam belched from the Sammath Naur, and the side of the cone was riven open, and a huge fiery vomit rolled in slow thunderous cascade down the eastern mountain-side.

Frodo and Sam could go no further. Their last strength of mind and body was swiftly ebbing. They had reached a low ashen hill piled at the Mountain's foot; but from it there was no more escape. It was an island now, not long to endure, amid the torment of Orodruin. All about it the earth gaped, and from deep rifts and pits smoke and fumes leaped up. Behind them the Mountain was convulsed. Great rents opened in its side. Slow rivers of fire came down the long slopes towards them. Soon they would be engulfed. A rain of hot ash was falling.

They stood now; and Sam still holding his master's hand caressed it. He sighed. 'What a tale we have been in, Mr. Frodo, haven't we?' he said. 'I wish I could hear it told! Do you think they'll say: *Now comes the story of Nine-fingered Frodo and the Ring of Doom*? And then everyone will hush, like we did, when in Rivendell they told us the tale of Beren One-hand and the Great Jewel. I wish I could hear it! And I wonder how it will go on after our part.'

But even while he spoke so, to keep fear away until the very last, his eyes still strayed north, north into the eye of the wind, to where the sky far off was clear, as the cold blast, rising to a gale, drove back the darkness and the ruin of the clouds.

And so it was that Gwaihir saw them with his keen far-seeing eyes, as down the wild wind he came, and daring the great peril of the skies he circled in the air: two small dark figures, forlorn, hand in hand upon a little hill, while the world shook under them, and gasped, and rivers of fire drew near. And even as he espied them and came swooping down, he saw them fall, worn out, or choked with fumes and heat, or stricken down by despair at last, hiding their eyes from death.

Side by side they lay; and down swept Gwaihir, and down came Landroval and Meneldor the swift; and in a dream, not knowing what fate had befallen them, the wanderers were lifted up and borne far away out of the darkness and the fire.

When Sam awoke, he found that he was lying on some soft bed, but over him gently swayed wide beechen boughs, and through their young leaves sunlight glimmered, green and gold. All the air was full of a sweet mingled scent.

He remembered that smell: the fragrance of Ithilien. 'Bless me!' he mused. 'How long have I been asleep?' For the scent had borne him back to the day when he had lit his little fire under the sunny bank; and for the moment all else between was out of waking memory. He stretched and drew a deep breath. 'Why, what a dream I've had!' he muttered. 'I am glad to wake!' He sat up and then he saw that Frodo was lying beside him, and slept peacefully, one hand behind his head, and the other resting upon the coverlet. It was the right hand, and the third finger was missing.

Full memory flooded back, and Sam cried aloud: 'It wasn't
a dream! Then where are we?'

And a voice spoke softly behind him: 'In the land of
Ithilien, and in the keeping of the King; and he awaits you.'
With that Gandalf stood before him, robed in white, his
beard now gleaming like pure snow in the twinkling of the
leafy sunlight. 'Well, Master Samwise, how do you feel?' he
said.

But Sam lay back, and stared with open mouth, and for a
moment, between bewilderment and great joy, he could not
answer. At last he gasped: 'Gandalf! I thought you were
dead! But then I thought I was dead myself. Is everything
sad going to come untrue? What's happened to the world?'

'A great Shadow has departed,' said Gandalf, and then he
laughed, and the sound was like music, or like water in a
parched land; and as he listened the thought came to Sam
that he had not heard laughter, the pure sound of merriment,
for days upon days without count. It fell upon his ears like
the echo of all the joys he had ever known. But he himself
burst into tears. Then, as a sweet rain will pass down a wind
of spring and the sun will shine out the clearer, his tears
ceased, and his laughter welled up, and laughing he sprang
from his bed.

'How do I feel?' he cried. 'Well, I don't know how to say
it. I feel, I feel' – he waved his arms in the air – 'I feel like
spring after winter, and sun on the leaves; and like trumpets
and harps and all the songs I have ever heard!' He stopped
and he turned towards his master. 'But how's Mr. Frodo?'
he said. 'Isn't it a shame about his poor hand? But I hope
he's all right otherwise. He's had a cruel time.'

'Yes, I am all right otherwise,' said Frodo, sitting up and
laughing in his turn. 'I fell asleep again waiting for you, Sam,
you sleepy-head. I was awake early this morning, and now
it must be nearly noon.'

'Noon?' said Sam, trying to calculate. 'Noon of what
day?'

'The fourteenth of the New Year,' said Gandalf; 'or if you

like, the eighth day of April in the Shire reckoning.* But in Gondor the New Year will always now begin upon the twenty-fifth of March when Sauron fell, and when you were brought out of the fire to the King. He has tended you, and now he awaits you. You shall eat and drink with him. When you are ready I will lead you to him.'

'The King?' said Sam. 'What king, and who is he?'

'The King of Gondor and Lord of the Western Lands,' said Gandalf; 'and he has taken back all his ancient realm. He will ride soon to his crowning, but he waits for you.'

'What shall we wear?' said Sam; for all he could see was the old and tattered clothes that they had journeyed in, lying folded on the ground beside their beds.

'The clothes that you wore on your way to Mordor,' said Gandalf. 'Even the orc-rags that you bore in the black land, Frodo, shall be preserved. No silks and linens, nor any armour or heraldry could be more honourable. But later I will find some other clothes, perhaps.'

Then he held out his hands to them, and they saw that one shone with light. 'What have you got there?' Frodo cried. 'Can it be – ?'

'Yes, I have brought your two treasures. They were found on Sam when you were rescued; the Lady Galadriel's gifts: your glass, Frodo; and your box, Sam. You will be glad to have these safe again.'

When they were washed and clad, and had eaten a light meal, the Hobbits followed Gandalf. They stepped out of the beech-grove in which they had lain, and passed on to a long green lawn, glowing in sunshine, bordered by stately dark-leaved trees laden with scarlet blossom. Behind them they could hear the sound of falling water, and a stream ran down before them between flowering banks, until it came to a greenwood at the lawn's foot and passed then on under an

---

* There were thirty days in March (or Rethe) in the Shire calendar.

archway of trees, through which they saw the shimmer of water far away.

As they came to the opening in the wood, they were surprised to see knights in bright mail and tall guards in silver and black standing there, who greeted them with honour and bowed before them. And then one blew a long trumpet, and they went on through the aisle of trees beside the singing stream. So they came to a wide green land, and beyond it was a broad river in a silver haze, out of which rose a long wooded isle, and many ships lay by its shores. But on the field where they now stood a great host was drawn up, in ranks and companies glittering in the sun. And as the Hobbits approached swords were unsheathed, and spears were shaken, and horns and trumpets sang, and men cried with many voices and in many tongues:

> 'Long live the Halflings! Praise them with great praise!
> Cuio i Pheriain anann! Aglar'ni Pheriannath!
> Praise them with great praise, Frodo and Samwise!
> Daur a Berhael, Conin en Annûn! Eglerio!
> Praise them!
> Eglerio!
> A laita te, laita te! Andave laituvalmet!
> Praise them!
> Cormacolindor, a laita tárienna!
> Praise them! The Ring-bearers, praise them with great
> praise!'

And so the red blood blushing in their faces and their eyes shining with wonder, Frodo and Sam went forward and saw that amidst the clamorous host were set three high-seats built of green turves. Behind the seat upon the right floated, white on green, a great horse running free; upon the left was a banner, silver upon blue, a ship swan-prowed faring on the sea; but behind the highest throne in the midst of all a great standard was spread in the breeze, and there a white tree flowered upon a sable field beneath a shining crown and seven glittering stars. On the throne sat a mail-clad man, a great sword was laid across his knees, but he wore no helm. As they drew near he rose. And then they knew him, changed as he was, so high and glad of face, kingly, lord of Men, dark-haired with eyes of grey.

Frodo ran to meet him, and Sam followed close behind. 'Well, if this isn't the crown of all!' he said. 'Strider, or I'm still asleep!'

'Yes, Sam, Strider,' said Aragorn. 'It is a long way, is it not, from Bree, where you did not like the look of me? A long way for us all, but yours has been the darkest road.'

And then to Sam's surprise and utter confusion he bowed his knee before them; and taking them by the hand, Frodo upon his right and Sam upon his left, he led them to the throne, and setting them upon it, he turned to the men and captains who stood by and spoke, so that his voice rang over all the host, crying:

'Praise them with great praise!'

And when the glad shout had swelled up and died away again, to Sam's final and complete satisfaction and pure joy, a minstrel of Gondor stood forth, and knelt, and begged leave to sing. And behold! he said:

'Lo! lords and knights and men of valour unashamed, kings and princes, and fair people of Gondor, and Riders of Rohan, and ye sons of Elrond, and Dúnedain of the North, and Elf and Dwarf, and greathearts of the Shire, and all free folk of the West, now listen to my lay. For I will sing to you of Frodo of the Nine Fingers and the Ring of Doom.'

And when Sam heard that he laughed aloud for sheer delight, and he stood up and cried: 'O great glory and splendour! And all my wishes have come true!' And then he wept.

And all the host laughed and wept, and in the midst of their merriment and tears the clear voice of the minstrel rose like silver and gold, and all men were hushed. And he sang to them, now in the Elven-tongue, now in the speech of the West, until their hearts, wounded with sweet words, over-flowed, and their joy was like swords, and they passed in thought out to regions where pain and delight flow together and tears are the very wine of blessedness.

And at the last, as the Sun fell from the noon and the shadows of the trees lengthened, he ended. 'Praise them with great praise!' he said and knelt. And then Aragorn stood up, and all the host arose, and they passed to pavilions made ready, to eat and drink and make merry while the day lasted.

Frodo and Sam were led apart and brought to a tent, and there their old raiment was taken off, but folded and set aside with honour; and clean linen was given to them. Then Gandalf came and in his arms, to the wonder of Frodo, he bore the sword and the elven-cloak and the mithril-coat that had been taken from him in Mordor. For Sam he brought a coat of gilded mail, and his elven-cloak all healed of the soils and hurts that it had suffered; and then he laid before them two swords.

'I do not wish for any sword,' said Frodo.

'Tonight at least you should wear one,' said Gandalf.

Then Frodo took the small sword that had belonged to Sam, and had been laid at his side in Cirith Ungol. 'Sting I gave to you Sam,' he said.

'No, master! Mr. Bilbo gave it to you, and it goes with his silver coat; he would not wish anyone else to wear it now.'

Frodo gave way; and Gandalf, as if he were their esquire, knelt and girt the sword-belts about them, and then rising he set circlets of silver upon their heads. And when they were arrayed they went to the great feast; and they sat at the King's table with Gandalf, and King Éomer of Rohan, and the Prince Imrahil and all the chief captains; and there also were Gimli and Legolas.

But when, after the Standing Silence, wine was brought there came in two esquires to serve the kings; or so they seemed to be: one was clad in the silver and sable of the Guards of Minas Tirith, and the other in white and green. But Sam wondered what such young boys were doing in an army of mighty men. Then suddenly as they drew near and he could see them plainly, he exclaimed:

'Why, look Mr. Frodo! Look here! Well, if it isn't Pippin. Mr. Peregrin Took I should say, and Mr. Merry! How they have grown! Bless me! But I can see there's more tales to tell than ours.'

'There are indeed,' said Pippin turning towards him. 'And we'll begin telling them, as soon as this feast is ended. In the meantime you can try Gandalf. He's not so close as he used to be, though he laughs now more than he talks. For the present Merry and I are busy. We are knights of the City and of the Mark, as I hope you observe.'

At last the glad day ended; and when the Sun was gone and the round Moon rode slowly above the mists of Anduin and flickered through the fluttering leaves, Frodo and Sam sat under the whispering trees amid the fragrance of fair Ithilien; and they talked deep into the night with Merry and Pippin and Gandalf, and after a while Legolas and Gimli joined them. There Frodo and Sam learned much of all that had happened to the Company after their fellowship was broken on the evil day at Parth Galen by Rauros Falls; and still there was always more to ask and more to tell.

Orcs, and talking trees, and leagues of grass, and galloping riders, and glittering caves, and white towers and golden halls, and battles, and tall ships sailing, all these passed before Sam's mind until he felt bewildered. But amidst all these wonders he returned always to his astonishment at the size of Merry and Pippin; and he made them stand back to back with Frodo and himself. He scratched his head. 'Can't understand it at your age!' he said. 'But there it is: you're three inches taller than you ought to be, or I'm a dwarf.'

'That you certainly are not,' said Gimli. 'But what did I say? Mortals cannot go drinking ent-draughts and expect no more to come of them than of a pot of beer.'

'Ent-draughts?' said Sam. 'There you go about Ents again;

but what they are beats me. Why, it will take weeks before we get all these things sized up!'

'Weeks indeed,' said Pippin. 'And then Frodo will have to be locked up in a tower in Minas Tirith and write it all down. Otherwise he will forget half of it, and poor old Bilbo will be dreadfully disappointed.'

At length Gandalf rose. 'The hands of the King are hands of healing, dear friends,' he said. 'But you went to the very brink of death ere he recalled you, putting forth all his power, and sent you into the sweet forgetfulness of sleep. And though you have indeed slept long and blessedly, still it is now time to sleep again.'

'And not only Sam and Frodo here,' said Gimli, 'but you too, Pippin. I love you, if only because of the pains you have cost me, which I shall never forget. Nor shall I forget finding you on the hill of the last battle. But for Gimli the Dwarf you would have been lost then. But at least I know now the look of a hobbit's foot, though it be all that can be seen under a heap of bodies. And when I heaved that great carcase off you, I made sure you were dead. I could have torn out my beard. And it is only a day yet since you were first up and abroad again. To bed now you go. And so shall I.'

'And I,' said Legolas, 'shall walk in the woods of this fair land, which is rest enough. In days to come, if my Elven-lord allows, some of our folk shall remove hither; and when we come it shall be blessed, for a while. For a while: a month, a life, a hundred years of Men. But Anduin is near, and Anduin leads down to the Sea. To the Sea!

> To the Sea, to the Sea! The white gulls are crying,
> The wind is blowing, and the white foam is flying.
> West, west away, the round sun is falling.
> Grey ship, grey ship, do you hear them calling,
> The voices of my people that have gone before me?
> I will leave, I will leave the woods that bore me;
> For our days are ending and our years failing.

I will pass the wide waters lonely sailing.
Long are the waves on the Last Shore falling,
Sweet are the voices in the Lost Isle calling,
In Eressëa, in Elvenhome that no man can discover,
Where the leaves fall not: land of my people for ever!'

And so singing Legolas went away down the hill.

Then the others also departed, and Frodo and Sam went to their beds and slept. And in the morning they rose again in hope and peace; and they spent many days in Ithilien. For the Field of Cormallen, where the host was now encamped, was near to Henneth Annûn, and the stream that flowed from its falls could be heard in the night as it rushed down through its rocky gate, and passed through the flowery meads into the tides of Anduin by the Isle of Cair Andros. The hobbits wandered here and there visiting again the places that they had passed before; and Sam hoped always in some shadow of the woods or secret glade to catch, maybe, a glimpse of the great Oliphaunt. And when he learned that at the siege of Gondor there had been a great number of these beasts but that they were all destroyed, he thought it a sad loss.

'Well, one can't be everywhere at once, I suppose,' he said. 'But I missed a lot, seemingly.'

In the meanwhile the host made ready for the return to Minas Tirith. The weary rested and the hurt were healed. For some had laboured and fought much with the remnants of the Easterlings and Southrons, until all were subdued. And, latest of all, those returned who had passed into Mordor and destroyed the fortresses in the north of the land.

But at the last when the month of May was drawing near the Captains of the West set out again; and they went aboard ship with all their men, and they sailed from Cair Andros down Anduin to Osgiliath; and there they remained for one day; and the day after they came to the green fields of the

Pelennor and saw again the white towers under tall Mindolluin, the City of the Men of Gondor, last memory of Westernesse, that had passed through the darkness and fire to a new day.

And there in the midst of the fields they set up their pavilions and awaited the morning; for it was the Eve of May, and the King would enter his gates with the rising of the Sun.

CHAPTER V

THE STEWARD AND THE KING

Over the city of Gondor doubt and great dread had hung. Fair weather and clear sun had seemed but a mockery to men whose days held little hope, and who looked each morning for news of doom. Their lord was dead and burned, dead lay the King of Rohan in their citadel, and the new king that had come to them in the night was gone again to a war with powers too dark and terrible for any might or valour to conquer. And no news came. After the host left Morgul Vale and took the northward road beneath the shadow of the mountains no messenger had returned nor any rumour of what was passing in the brooding East.

When the Captains were but two days gone, the Lady Éowyn bade the women who tended her to bring her raiment, and she would not be gainsaid, but rose; and when they had clothed her and set her arm in a sling of linen, she went to the Warden of the Houses of Healing.

'Sir,' she said, 'I am in great unrest, and I cannot lie longer in sloth.'

'Lady,' he answered, 'you are not yet healed, and I was commanded to tend you with especial care. You should not have risen from your bed for seven days yet, or so I was bidden. I beg you to go back.'

'I am healed,' she said, 'healed at least in body, save my left arm only, and that is at ease. But I shall sicken anew, if there is naught that I can do. Are there no tidings of war? The women can tell me nothing.'

'There are no tidings,' said the Warden, 'save that the Lords have ridden to Morgul Vale; and men say that the new captain out of the North is their chief. A great lord is that, and a healer; and it is a thing passing strange to me that the

healing hand should also wield the sword. It is not thus in
Gondor now, though once it was so, if old tales be true. But
for long years we healers have only sought to patch the rents
made by the men of swords. Though we should still have
enough to do without them: the world is full enough of hurts
and mischances without wars to multiply them.'

'It needs but one foe to breed a war, not two, Master
Warden,' answered Éowyn. 'And those who have not swords
can still die upon them. Would you have the folk of Gondor
gather you herbs only, when the Dark Lord gathers armies?
And it is not always good to be healed in body. Nor is it always
evil to die in battle, even in bitter pain. Were I permitted, in
this dark hour I would choose the latter.'

The Warden looked at her. Tall she stood there, her eyes
bright in her white face, her hand clenched as she turned
and gazed out of his window that opened to the East. He
sighed and shook his head. After a pause she turned to him
again.

'Is there no deed to do?' she said. 'Who commands in this
City?'

'I do not rightly know,' he answered. 'Such things are not
my care. There is a marshal over the Riders of Rohan; and
the Lord Húrin, I am told, commands the men of Gondor.
But the Lord Faramir is by right the Steward of the City.'

'Where can I find him?'

'In this house, lady. He was sorely hurt, but is now set
again on the way to health. But I do not know——'

'Will you not bring me to him? Then you will know.'

The Lord Faramir was walking alone in the garden of the
Houses of Healing, and the sunlight warmed him, and he
felt life run new in his veins; but his heart was heavy, and he
looked out over the walls eastward. And coming, the Warden
spoke his name, and he turned and saw the Lady Éowyn of
Rohan; and he was moved with pity, for he saw that she was
hurt, and his clear sight perceived her sorrow and unrest.

'My lord,' said the Warden, 'here is the Lady Éowyn of

Rohan. She rode with the king and was sorely hurt, and dwells now in my keeping. But she is not content, and she wishes to speak to the Steward of the City.'

'Do not misunderstand him, lord,' said Éowyn. 'It is not lack of care that grieves me. No houses could be fairer, for those who desire to be healed. But I cannot lie in sloth, idle, caged. I looked for death in battle. But I have not died, and battle still goes on.'

At a sign from Faramir, the Warden bowed and departed. 'What would you have me do, lady?' said Faramir. 'I also am a prisoner of the healers.' He looked at her, and being a man whom pity deeply stirred, it seemed to him that her loveliness amid her grief would pierce his heart. And she looked at him and saw the grave tenderness in his eyes, and yet knew, for she was bred among men of war, that here was one whom no Rider of the Mark would outmatch in battle.

'What do you wish?' he said again. 'If it lies in my power, I will do it.'

'I would have you command this Warden, and bid him let me go,' she said; but though her words were still proud, her heart faltered, and for the first time she doubted herself. She guessed that this tall man, both stern and gentle, might think her merely wayward, like a child that has not the firmness of mind to go on with a dull task to the end.

'I myself am in the Warden's keeping,' answered Faramir. 'Nor have I yet taken up my authority in the City. But had I done so, I should still listen to his counsel, and should not cross his will in matters of his craft, unless in some great need.'

'But I do not desire healing,' she said. 'I wish to ride to war like my brother Éomer, or better like Théoden the king, for he died and has both honour and peace.'

'It is too late, lady, to follow the Captains, even if you had the strength,' said Faramir. 'But death in battle may come to us all yet, willing or unwilling. You will be better prepared to face it in your own manner, if while there is still time you do as the Healer commanded. You and I, we must endure with patience the hours of waiting.'

She did not answer, but as he looked at her it seemed to him that something in her softened, as though a bitter frost were yielding at the first faint presage of Spring. A tear sprang in her eye and fell down her cheek, like a glistening rain-drop. Her proud head drooped a little. Then quietly, more as if speaking to herself than to him: 'But the healers would have me lie abed seven days yet,' she said. 'And my window does not look eastward.' Her voice was now that of a maiden young and sad.

Faramir smiled, though his heart was filled with pity. 'Your window does not look eastward?' he said. 'That can be amended. In this I will command the Warden. If you will stay in this house in our care, lady, and take your rest, then you shall walk in this garden in the sun, as you will; and you shall look east, whither all our hopes have gone. And here you will find me, walking and waiting, and also looking east. It would ease my care, if you would speak to me, or walk at whiles with me.'

Then she raised her head and looked him in the eyes again; and a colour came in her pale face. 'How should I ease your care, my lord?' she said. 'And I do not desire the speech of living men.'

'Would you have my plain answer?' he said.

'I would.'

'Then, Éowyn of Rohan, I say to you that you are beautiful. In the valleys of our hills there are flowers fair and bright, and maidens fairer still; but neither flower nor lady have I seen till now in Gondor so lovely, and so sorrowful. It may be that only a few days are left ere darkness falls upon our world, and when it comes I hope to face it steadily; but it would ease my heart, if while the Sun yet shines, I could see you still. For you and I have both passed under the wings of the Shadow, and the same hand drew us back.'

'Alas, not me, lord!' she said. 'Shadow lies on me still. Look not to me for healing! I am a shieldmaiden and my hand is ungentle. But I thank you for this at least, that I need not keep to my chamber. I will walk abroad by the grace of the Steward of the City.' And she did him a courtesy and walked back to the house. But Faramir for a long while walked alone in the garden, and his glance now strayed rather to the house than to the eastward walls.

When he returned to his chamber he called for the Warden, and heard all that he could tell of the Lady of Rohan.

'But I doubt not, lord,' said the Warden, 'that you would learn more from the Halfling that is with us; for he was in the riding of the king, and with the Lady at the end, they say.'

And so Merry was sent to Faramir, and while that day lasted they talked long together, and Faramir learned much, more even than Merry put into words; and he thought that he understood now something of the grief and unrest of Éowyn of Rohan. And in the fair evening Faramir and Merry walked in the garden, but she did not come.

But in the morning, as Faramir came from the Houses, he saw her, as she stood upon the walls; and she was clad all in white, and gleamed in the sun. And he called to her, and she came down, and they walked on the grass or sat under a green tree together, now in silence, now in speech. And each day after they did likewise. And the Warden looking from his window was glad in heart, for he was a healer, and his care was lightened; and certain it was that, heavy as was the dread and foreboding of those days upon the hearts of men, still these two of his charges prospered and grew daily in strength.

And so the fifth day came since the Lady Éowyn went first to Faramir; and they stood now together once more upon the walls of the City and looked out. No tidings had yet come, and all hearts were darkened. The weather, too, was bright no longer. It was cold. A wind that had sprung up in the night was blowing now keenly from the North, and it was rising; but the lands about looked grey and drear.

They were clad in warm raiment and heavy cloaks, and over all the Lady Éowyn wore a great blue mantle of the colour of deep summer-night, and it was set with silver stars about hem and throat. Faramir had sent for this robe and had wrapped it about her; and he thought that she looked fair and queenly indeed as she stood there at his side. The mantle was wrought for his mother, Finduilas of Amroth, who died untimely, and was to him but a memory of loveliness in far days and of his first grief; and her robe seemed to him raiment fitting for the beauty and sadness of Éowyn.

But she now shivered beneath the starry mantle, and she looked northward, above the grey hither lands, into the eye of the cold wind where far away the sky was hard and clear.

'What do you look for, Éowyn?' said Faramir.

'Does not the Black Gate lie yonder?' said she. 'And must he not now be come thither? It is seven days since he rode away.'

'Seven days,' said Faramir. 'But think not ill of me, if I say to you: they have brought me both a joy and a pain that I never thought to know. Joy to see you; but pain, because now the fear and doubt of this evil time are grown dark indeed. Éowyn, I would not have this world end now, or lose so soon what I have found.'

'Lose what you have found, lord?' she answered; but she looked at him gravely and her eyes were kind. 'I know not what in these days you have found that you could lose. But come, my friend, let us not speak of it! Let us not speak at all! I stand upon some dreadful brink, and it is utterly dark in the abyss before my feet, but whether there is any light behind me I cannot tell. For I cannot turn yet. I wait for some stroke of doom.'

'Yes, we wait for the stroke of doom,' said Faramir. And they said no more; and it seemed to them as they stood upon the wall that the wind died, and the light failed, and the Sun was bleared, and all sounds in the City or in the lands about were hushed: neither wind, nor voice, nor bird-call, nor rustle of leaf, nor their own breath could be heard; the very beating of their hearts was stilled. Time halted.

And as they stood so, their hands met and clasped, though they did not know it. And still they waited for they knew not what. Then presently it seemed to them that above the ridges of the distant mountains another vast mountain of darkness rose, towering up like a wave that should engulf the world, and about it lightnings flickered; and then a tremor ran through the earth, and they felt the walls of the City quiver. A sound like a sigh went up from all the lands about them; and their hearts beat suddenly again.

'It reminds me of Númenor,' said Faramir, and wondered to hear himself speak.

'Of Númenor?' said Éowyn.

'Yes,' said Faramir, 'of the land of Westernesse that foundered, and of the great dark wave climbing over the green lands and above the hills, and coming on, darkness unescapable. I often dream of it.'

'Then you think that the Darkness is coming?' said Éowyn. 'Darkness Unescapable?' And suddenly she drew close to him.

'No,' said Faramir, looking into her face. 'It was but a picture in the mind. I do not know what is happening. The reason of my waking mind tells me that great evil has befallen and we stand at the end of days. But my heart says nay; and all my limbs are light, and a hope and joy are come to me that no reason can deny. Éowyn, Éowyn, White Lady of Rohan, in this hour I do not believe that any darkness will endure!' And he stooped and kissed her brow.

And so they stood on the walls of the City of Gondor, and a great wind rose and blew, and their hair, raven and golden, streamed out mingling in the air. And the Shadow departed, and the Sun was unveiled, and light leaped forth; and the waters of Anduin shone like silver, and in all the houses of the City men sang for the joy that welled up in their hearts from what source they could not tell.

And before the Sun had fallen far from the noon out of

the East there came a great Eagle flying, and he bore tidings
beyond hope from the Lords of the West, crying:

> *Sing now, ye people of the Tower of Anor,*
> *for the Realm of Sauron is ended for ever,*
>   *and the Dark Tower is thrown down.*

> *Sing and rejoice, ye people of the Tower of Guard,*
> *for your watch hath not been in vain,*
> *and the Black Gate is broken,*
> *and your King hath passed through,*
>   *and he is victorious.*

> *Sing and be glad, all ye children of the West,*
> *for your King shall come again,*
> *and he shall dwell among you*
>   *all the days of your life.*

> *And the Tree that was withered shall be renewed,*
> *and he shall plant it in the high places,*
>   *and the City shall be blessed.*

>   *Sing all ye people!*

And the people sang in all the ways of the City.

The days that followed were golden, and Spring and Summer joined and made revel together in the fields of Gondor.
And tidings now came by swift riders from Cair Andros of
all that was done, and the City made ready for the coming
of the King. Merry was summoned and rode away with the
wains that took store of goods to Osgiliath and thence by
ship to Cair Andros; but Faramir did not go, for now being
healed he took upon him his authority and the Stewardship,
although it was only for a little while, and his duty was to
prepare for one who should replace him.

And Éowyn did not go, though her brother sent word

begging her to come to the field of Cormallen. And Faramir wondered at this, but he saw her seldom, being busy with many matters; and she dwelt still in the Houses of Healing and walked alone in the garden, and her face grew pale again, and it seemed that in all the City she only was ailing and sorrowful. And the Warden of the Houses was troubled, and he spoke to Faramir.

Then Faramir came and sought her, and once more they stood on the walls together; and he said to her: 'Éowyn, why do you tarry here, and do not go to the rejoicing in Cormallen beyond Cair Andros, where your brother awaits you?'

And she said: 'Do you not know?'

But he answered: 'Two reasons there may be, but which is true, I do not know.'

And she said: 'I do not wish to play at riddles. Speak plainer!'

'Then if you will have it so, lady,' he said: 'you do not go, because only your brother called for you, and to look on the Lord Aragorn, Elendil's heir, in his triumph would now bring you no joy. Or because I do not go, and you desire still to be near me. And maybe for both these reasons, and you yourself cannot choose between them. Éowyn, do you not love me, or will you not?'

'I wished to be loved by another,' she answered. 'But I desire no man's pity.'

'That I know,' he said. 'You desired to have the love of the Lord Aragorn. Because he was high and puissant, and you wished to have renown and glory and to be lifted far above the mean things that crawl on the earth. And as a great captain may to a young soldier he seemed to you admirable. For so he is, a lord among men, the greatest that now is. But when he gave you only understanding and pity, then you desired to have nothing, unless a brave death in battle. Look at me, Éowyn!'

And Éowyn looked at Faramir long and steadily; and Faramir said: 'Do not scorn pity that is the gift of a gentle heart, Éowyn! But I do not offer you my pity. For you are a lady high and valiant and have yourself won renown that shall not be forgotten; and you are a lady beautiful, I deem, beyond even the words of the Elven-tongue to tell. And I love you. Once I pitied your sorrow. But now, were you sorrowless, without fear or any lack, were you the blissful Queen of Gondor, still I would love you. Éowyn, do you not love me?'

Then the heart of Éowyn changed, or else at last she understood it. And suddenly her winter passed, and the sun shone on her.

'I stand in Minas Anor, the Tower of the Sun,' she said; 'and behold! the Shadow has departed! I will be a shieldmaiden no longer, nor vie with the great Riders, nor take joy only in the songs of slaying. I will be a healer, and love all things that grow and are not barren.' And again she looked at Faramir. 'No longer do I desire to be a queen,' she said.

Then Faramir laughed merrily. 'That is well,' he said; 'for I am not a king. Yet I will wed with the White Lady of Rohan, if it be her will. And if she will, then let us cross the River and in happier days let us dwell in fair Ithilien and there make a garden. All things will grow with joy there, if the White Lady comes.'

'Then must I leave my own people, man of Gondor?' she said. 'And would you have your proud folk say of you: "There goes a lord who tamed a wild shieldmaiden of the North! Was there no woman of the race of Númenor to choose?"'

'I would,' said Faramir. And he took her in his arms and kissed her under the sunlit sky, and he cared not that they stood high upon the walls in the sight of many. And many indeed saw them and the light that shone about them as they came down from the walls and went hand in hand to the Houses of Healing.

And to the Warden of the Houses Faramir said: 'Here is the Lady Éowyn of Rohan, and now she is healed.'

And the Warden said: 'Then I release her from my charge

and bid her farewell, and may she suffer never hurt nor sickness again. I commend her to the care of the Steward of the City, until her brother returns.'

But Éowyn said: 'Yet now that I have leave to depart, I would remain. For this House has become to me of all dwellings the most blessed.' And she remained there until King Éomer came.

All things were now made ready in the City; and there was great concourse of people, for the tidings had gone out into all parts of Gondor, from Min-Rimmon even to Pinnath Gelin and the far coasts of the sea; and all that could come to the City made haste to come. And the City was filled again with women and fair children that returned to their homes laden with flowers; and from Dol Amroth came the harpers that harped most skilfully in all the land; and there were players upon viols and upon flutes and upon horns of silver, and clear-voiced singers from the vales of Lebennin.

At last an evening came when from the walls the pavilions could be seen upon the field, and all night lights were burning as men watched for the dawn. And when the sun rose in the clear morning above the mountains in the East, upon which shadows lay no more, then all the bells rang, and all the banners broke and flowed in the wind; and upon the White Tower of the citadel the standard of the Stewards, bright argent like snow in the sun, bearing no charge nor device, was raised over Gondor for the last time.

Now the Captains of the West led their host towards the City, and folk saw them advance in line upon line, flashing and glinting in the sunrise and rippling like silver. And so they came before the Gateway and halted a furlong from the walls. As yet no gates had been set up again, but a barrier was laid across the entrance to the City, and there stood men at arms in silver and black with long swords drawn. Before the barrier stood Faramir the Steward, and Húrin Warden of the Keys, and other captains of Gondor, and the Lady Éowyn of Rohan with Elfhelm the Marshal and many knights of the Mark; and upon either side of the Gate was a great press of fair people in raiment of many colours and garlands of flowers.

So now there was a wide space before the walls of Minas Tirith, and it was hemmed in upon all sides by the knights and the soldiers of Gondor and of Rohan, and by the people of the City and of all parts of the land. A hush fell upon all as out from the host stepped the Dúnedain in silver and grey; and before them came walking slow the Lord Aragorn. He was clad in black mail girt with silver, and he wore a long mantle of pure white clasped at the throat with a great jewel of green that shone from afar; but his head was bare save for a star upon his forehead bound by a slender fillet of silver. With him were Éomer of Rohan, and the Prince Imrahil, and Gandalf robed all in white, and four small figures that many men marvelled to see.

'Nay, cousin! they are not boys,' said Ioreth to her kinswoman from Imloth Melui, who stood beside her. 'Those are *Periain*, out of the far country of the Halflings, where they are princes of great fame, it is said. I should know, for I had one to tend in the Houses. They are small, but they are valiant. Why, cousin, one of them went with only his esquire into the Black Country and fought with the Dark Lord all by himself, and set fire to his Tower, if you can believe it. At least that is the tale in the City. That will be the one that walks with our Elfstone. They are dear friends, I hear. Now he is a marvel, the Lord Elfstone: not too soft in his speech, mind you, but he has a golden heart, as the saying is; and he has the healing hands. "The hands of the king are the hands of a healer", I said; and that was how it was all discovered. And Mithrandir, he said to me: "Ioreth, men will long remember your words", and———'

But Ioreth was not permitted to continue the instruction of her kinswoman from the country, for a single trumpet rang, and a dead silence followed. Then forth from the Gate went Faramir with Húrin of the Keys, and no others, save that behind them walked four men in the high helms and armour of the Citadel, and they bore a great casket of black *lebethron* bound with silver.

Faramir met Aragorn in the midst of those there assembled, and he knelt, and said: 'The last Steward of Gondor begs leave to surrender his office.' And he held out a white rod; but Aragorn took the rod and gave it back, saying: 'That office is not ended, and it shall be thine and thy heirs' as long as my line shall last. Do now thy office!'

Then Faramir stood up and spoke in a clear voice: 'Men of Gondor, hear now the Steward of this Realm! Behold! one has come to claim the kingship again at last. Here is Aragorn son of Arathorn, chieftain of the Dúnedain of Arnor, Captain of the Host of the West, bearer of the Star of the North, wielder of the Sword Reforged, victorious in battle, whose hands bring healing, the Elfstone, Elessar of the line of Valandil, Isildur's son, Elendil's son of Númenor. Shall he be king and enter into the City and dwell there?'

And all the host and all the people cried *yea* with one voice.

And Ioreth said to her kinswoman: 'This is just a ceremony such as we have in the City, cousin; for he has already entered, as I was telling you; and he said to me———' And then again she was obliged to silence, for Faramir spoke again.

'Men of Gondor, the loremasters tell that it was the custom of old that the king should receive the crown from his father ere he died; or if that might not be, that he should go alone and take it from the hands of his father in the tomb where he was laid. But since things must now be done otherwise, using the authority of the Steward, I have today brought hither from Rath Dínen the crown of Eärnur the last king, whose days passed in the time of our longfathers of old.'

Then the guards stepped forward, and Faramir opened the casket, and he held up an ancient crown. It was shaped like the helms of the Guards of the Citadel, save that it was loftier, and it was all white, and the wings at either side were wrought of pearl and silver in the likeness of the wings of a sea-bird, for it was the emblem of kings who came over the

Sea; and seven gems of adamant were set in the circlet, and upon its summit was set a single jewel the light of which went up like a flame.

Then Aragorn took the crown and held it up and said:

Et Eärello Endorenna utúlien. Sinome maruvan ar Hildinyar tenn' Ambar-metta!

And those were the words that Elendil spoke when he came up out of the Sea on the wings of the wind: 'Out of the Great Sea to Middle-earth I am come. In this place will I abide, and my heirs, unto the ending of the world.'

Then to the wonder of many Aragorn did not put the crown upon his head, but gave it back to Faramir, and said: 'By the labour and valour of many I have come into my inheritance. In token of this I would have the Ring-bearer bring the crown to me, and let Mithrandir set it upon my head, if he will; for he has been the mover of all that has been accomplished, and this is his victory.'

Then Frodo came forward and took the crown from Faramir and bore it to Gandalf; and Aragorn knelt, and Gandalf set the White Crown upon his head, and said:

'Now come the days of the King, and may they be blessed while the thrones of the Valar endure!'

But when Aragorn arose all that beheld him gazed in silence, for it seemed to them that he was revealed to them now for the first time. Tall as the sea-kings of old, he stood above all that were near; ancient of days he seemed and yet in the flower of manhood; and wisdom sat upon his brow, and strength and healing were in his hands, and a light was about him. And then Faramir cried:

'Behold the King!'

And in that moment all the trumpets were blown, and the King Elessar went forth and came to the barrier, and Húrin of the Keys thrust it back; and amid the music of harp and of viol and of flute and the singing of clear voices the King passed through the flower-laden streets, and came to the Citadel, and entered in; and the banner of the Tree and the Stars was unfurled upon the topmost tower, and the reign of King Elessar began, of which many songs have told.

In his time the City was made more fair than it had ever been, even in the days of its first glory; and it was filled with trees and with fountains, and its gates were wrought of mithril and steel, and its streets were paved with white marble; and the Folk of the Mountain laboured in it, and the Folk of the Wood rejoiced to come there; and all was healed and made good, and the houses were filled with men and women and the laughter of children, and no window was blind nor any courtyard empty; and after the ending of the Third Age of the world into the new age it preserved the memory and the glory of the years that were gone.

In the days that followed his crowning the King sat on his throne in the Hall of the Kings and pronounced his judgements. And embassies came from many lands and peoples, from the East and the South, and from the borders of Mirkwood, and from Dunland in the west. And the King pardoned the Easterlings that had given themselves up, and sent them away free, and he made peace with the peoples of Harad; and the slaves of Mordor he released and gave to them all the lands about Lake Núrnen to be their own. And there were brought before him many to receive his praise and reward for their valour; and last the captain of the Guard brought to him Beregond to be judged.

And the King said to Beregond: 'Beregond, by your sword blood was spilled in the Hallows, where that is forbidden. Also you left your post without leave of Lord or of Captain. For these things, of old, death was the penalty. Now therefore I must pronounce your doom.

'All penalty is remitted for your valour in battle, and still more because all that you did was for the love of the Lord Faramir. Nonetheless you must leave the Guard of the Citadel, and you must go forth from the City of Minas Tirith.'

Then the blood left Beregond's face, and he was stricken to the heart and bowed his head. But the King said:

'So it must be, for you are appointed to the White

Company, the Guard of Faramir, Prince of Ithilien, and you shall be its captain and dwell in Emyn Arnen in honour and peace, and in the service of him for whom you risked all, to save him from death.'

And then Beregond, perceiving the mercy and justice of the King, was glad, and kneeling kissed his hand, and departed in joy and content. And Aragorn gave to Faramir Ithilien to be his princedom, and bade him dwell in the hills of Emyn Arnen within sight of the City.

'For,' said he, 'Minas Ithil in Morgul Vale shall be utterly destroyed, and though it may in time to come be made clean, no man may dwell there for many long years.'

And last of all Aragorn greeted Éomer of Rohan, and they embraced, and Aragorn said: 'Between us there can be no word of giving or taking, nor of reward; for we are brethren. In happy hour did Eorl ride from the North, and never has any league of peoples been more blessed, so that neither has ever failed the other, nor shall fail. Now, as you know, we have laid Théoden the Renowned in a tomb in the Hallows, and there he shall lie for ever among the Kings of Gondor, if you will. Or if you desire it, we will come to Rohan and bring him back to rest with his own people.'

And Éomer answered: 'Since the day when you rose before me out of the green grass of the downs I have loved you, and that love shall not fail. But now I must depart for a while to my own realm, where there is much to heal and set in order. But as for the Fallen, when all is made ready we will return for him; but here let him sleep a while.'

And Éowyn said to Faramir: 'Now I must go back to my own land and look on it once again, and help my brother in his labour; but when one whom I long loved as father is laid at last to rest, I will return.'

So the glad days passed; and on the eighth day of May the Riders of Rohan made ready, and rode off by the North-way, and with them went the sons of Elrond. All the road was lined with people to do them honour and praise them, from the Gate of the City to the walls of the Pelennor. Then all others that dwelt afar went back to their homes rejoicing; but in the City there was labour of many willing hands to rebuild and renew and to remove all the scars of war and the memory of the darkness.

The hobbits still remained in Minas Tirith, with Legolas and Gimli; for Aragorn was loth for the fellowship to be dissolved. 'At last all such things must end,' he said, 'but I would have you wait a little while longer: for the end of the deeds that you have shared in has not yet come. A day draws near that I have looked for in all the years of my manhood, and when it comes I would have my friends beside me.' But of that day he would say no more.

In those days the Companions of the Ring dwelt together in a fair house with Gandalf, and they went to and fro as they wished. And Frodo said to Gandalf: 'Do you know what this day is that Aragorn speaks of? For we are happy here, and I don't wish to go; but the days are running away, and Bilbo is waiting; and the Shire is my home.'

'As for Bilbo,' said Gandalf, 'he is waiting for the same day, and he knows what keeps you. And as for the passing of the days, it is now only May and high summer is not yet in; and though all things may seem changed, as if an age of the world had gone by, yet to the trees and the grass it is less than a year since you set out.'

'Pippin,' said Frodo, 'didn't you say that Gandalf was less close than of old? He was weary of his labours then, I think. Now he is recovering.'

And Gandalf said: 'Many folk like to know beforehand what is to be set on the table; but those who have laboured to prepare the feast like to keep their secret; for wonder makes the words of praise louder. And Aragorn himself waits for a sign.'

There came a day when Gandalf could not be found, and the Companions wondered what was going forward. But Gandalf took Aragorn out from the City by night, and he brought him to the southern feet of Mount Mindolluin; and there they found a path made in ages past that few now dared to tread. For it led up on to the mountain to a high hallow where only the kings had been wont to go. And they went up by steep ways, until they came to a high field below the snows that clad the lofty peaks, and it looked down over the precipice that stood behind the City. And standing there they surveyed the lands, for the morning was come; and they saw the towers of the City far below them like white pencils touched by the sunlight, and all the Vale of Anduin was like a garden, and the Mountains of Shadow were veiled in a golden mist. Upon the one side their sight reached to the grey Emyn Muil, and the glint of Rauros was like a star twinkling far off; and upon the other side they saw the River like a ribbon laid down to Pelargir, and beyond that was a light on the hem of the sky that spoke of the Sea.

And Gandalf said: 'This is your realm, and the heart of the greater realm that shall be. The Third Age of the world is ended, and the new age is begun; and it is your task to order its beginning and to preserve what may be preserved. For though much has been saved, much must now pass away; and the power of the Three Rings also is ended. And all the lands that you see, and those that lie round about them, shall be dwellings of Men. For the time comes of the Dominion of Men, and the Elder Kindred shall fade or depart.'

'I know it well, dear friend,' said Aragorn; 'but I would still have your counsel.'

'Not for long now,' said Gandalf. 'The Third Age was my age. I was the Enemy of Sauron; and my work is finished. I shall go soon. The burden must lie now upon you and your kindred.'

'But I shall die,' said Aragorn. 'For I am a mortal man, and though being what I am and of the race of the West unmingled, I shall have life far longer than other men, yet that is but a little while; and when those who are now in the wombs of women are born and have grown old, I too shall grow old. And who then shall govern Gondor and those who look to this City as to their queen, if my desire be not granted? The Tree in the Court of the Fountain is still withered and barren. When shall I see a sign that it will ever be otherwise?'

'Turn your face from the green world, and look where all seems barren and cold!' said Gandalf.

Then Aragorn turned, and there was a stony slope behind him running down from the skirts of the snow; and as he looked he was aware that alone there in the waste a growing thing stood. And he climbed to it, and saw that out of the very edge of the snow there sprang a sapling tree no more than three foot high. Already it had put forth young leaves long and shapely, dark above and silver beneath, and upon its slender crown it bore one small cluster of flowers whose white petals shone like the sunlit snow.

Then Aragorn cried: '*Yé! utúvienyes!* I have found it! Lo! here is a scion of the Eldest of Trees! But how comes it here? For it is not itself yet seven years old.'

And Gandalf coming looked at it, and said: 'Verily this is a sapling of the line of Nimloth the fair; and that was a seedling of Galathilion, and that a fruit of Telperion of many names, Eldest of Trees. Who shall say how it comes here in the appointed hour? But this is an ancient hallow, and ere the kings failed or the Tree withered in the court, a fruit must have been set here. For it is said that, though the fruit of the Tree comes seldom to ripeness, yet the life within may then lie sleeping through many long years, and none can foretell the time in which it will awake. Remember this. For if ever a fruit ripens, it should be planted, lest the line die out of the world. Here it has lain hidden on the mountain, even as the race of Elendil lay hidden in the wastes of the North. Yet the line of Nimloth is older far than your line, King Elessar.'

Then Aragorn laid his hand gently to the sapling, and lo! it seemed to hold only lightly to the earth, and it was removed without hurt; and Aragorn bore it back to the Citadel. Then the withered tree was uprooted, but with reverence; and they did not burn it, but laid it to rest in the silence of Rath

Dínen. And Aragorn planted the new tree in the court by
the fountain, and swiftly and gladly it began to grow; and
when the month of June entered in it was laden with blossom.

'The sign has been given,' said Aragorn, 'and the day is
not far off.' And he set watchmen upon the walls.

It was the day before Midsummer when messengers came
from Amon Dîn to the City, and they said that there was a
riding of fair folk out of the North, and they drew near now
to the walls of the Pelennor. And the King said: 'At last they
have come. Let all the City be made ready!'

Upon the very Eve of Midsummer, when the sky was blue
as sapphire and white stars opened in the East, but the West
was still golden, and the air was cool and fragrant, the riders
came down the North-way to the gates of Minas Tirith. First
rode Elrohir and Elladan with a banner of silver, and then
came Glorfindel and Erestor and all the household of Rivendell, and after them came the Lady Galadriel and Celeborn,
Lord of Lothlórien, riding upon white steeds and with them
many fair folk of their land, grey-cloaked with white gems in
their hair; and last came Master Elrond, mighty among Elves
and Men, bearing the sceptre of Annúminas, and beside him
upon a grey palfrey rode Arwen his daughter, Evenstar of
her people.

And Frodo when he saw her come glimmering in the
evening, with stars on her brow and a sweet fragrance about
her, was moved with great wonder, and he said to Gandalf:
'At last I understand why we have waited! This is the ending.
Now not day only shall be beloved, but night too shall be
beautiful and blessed and all its fear pass away!'

Then the King welcomed his guests, and they alighted;
and Elrond surrendered the sceptre, and laid the hand of his
daughter in the hand of the King, and together they went up
into the High City, and all the stars flowered in the sky. And
Aragorn the King Elessar wedded Arwen Undómiel in the
City of the Kings upon the day of Midsummer, and the tale
of their long waiting and labours was come to fulfilment.

CHAPTER VI

MANY PARTINGS

When the days of rejoicing were over at last the Companions thought of returning to their own homes. And Frodo went to the King as he was sitting with the Queen Arwen by the fountain, and she sang a song of Valinor, while the Tree grew and blossomed. They welcomed Frodo and rose to greet him; and Aragorn said:

'I know what you have come to say, Frodo: you wish to return to your own home. Well, dearest friend, the tree grows best in the land of its sires; but for you in all the lands of the West there will ever be a welcome. And though your people have had little fame in the legends of the great, they will now have more renown than many wide realms that are no more.'

'It is true that I wish to go back to the Shire,' said Frodo. 'But first I must go to Rivendell. For if there could be anything wanting in a time so blessed, I missed Bilbo; and I was grieved when among all the household of Elrond I saw that he was not come.'

'Do you wonder at that, Ring-bearer?' said Arwen. 'For you know the power of that thing which is now destroyed; and all that was done by that power is now passing away. But your kinsman possessed this thing longer than you. He is ancient in years now, according to his kind; and he awaits you, for he will not again make any long journey save one.'

'Then I beg leave to depart soon,' said Frodo.

'In seven days we will go,' said Aragorn. 'For we shall ride with you far on the road, even as far as the country of Rohan. In three days now Éomer will return hither to bear Théoden back to rest in the Mark, and we shall ride with him to honour the fallen. But now before you go I will confirm the words that Faramir spoke to you, and you are made free for ever of the realm of Gondor; and all your companions likewise. And if there were any gifts that I could give to match with your deeds you should have them; but whatever you desire you shall take with you, and you shall ride in honour and arrayed as princes of the land.'

But the Queen Arwen said: 'A gift I will give you. For I am the daughter of Elrond. I shall not go with him now when he departs to the Havens; for mine is the choice of Lúthien, and as she so have I chosen, both the sweet and the bitter. But in my stead you shall go, Ring-bearer, when the time comes, and if you then desire it. If your hurts grieve you still and the memory of your burden is heavy, then you may pass into the West, until all your wounds and weariness are healed. But wear this now in memory of Elfstone and Evenstar with whom your life has been woven!'

And she took a white gem like a star that lay upon her breast hanging upon a silver chain, and she set the chain about Frodo's neck. 'When the memory of the fear and the darkness troubles you,' she said, 'this will bring you aid.'

In three days, as the King had said, Éomer of Rohan came riding to the City, and with him came an *éored* of the fairest knights of the Mark. He was welcomed; and when they sat all at table in Merethrond, the Great Hall of Feasts, he beheld the beauty of the ladies that he saw and was filled with great wonder. And before he went to his rest he sent for Gimli the Dwarf, and he said to him: 'Gimli Glóin's son, have you your axe ready?'

'Nay, lord,' said Gimli, 'but I can speedily fetch it, if there be need.'

'You shall judge,' said Éomer. 'For there are certain rash words concerning the Lady in the Golden Wood that lie still between us. And now I have seen her with my eyes.'

'Well, lord,' said Gimli, 'and what say you now?'

'Alas!' said Éomer. 'I will not say that she is the fairest lady that lives.'

'Then I must go for my axe,' said Gimli.

'But first I will plead this excuse,' said Éomer. 'Had I seen her in other company, I would have said all that you could wish. But now I will put Queen Arwen Evenstar first, and I am ready to do battle on my own part with any who deny me. Shall I call for my sword?'

Then Gimli bowed low. 'Nay, you are excused for my part, lord,' he said. 'You have chosen the Evening; but my love is given to the Morning. And my heart forebodes that soon it will pass away for ever.'

At last the day of departure came, and a great and fair company made ready to ride north from the City. Then the kings of Gondor and Rohan went to the Hallows and they came to the tombs in Rath Dínen, and they bore away King Théoden upon a golden bier, and passed through the City in silence. Then they laid the bier upon a great wain with Riders of Rohan all about it and his banner borne before; and Merry being Théoden's esquire rode upon the wain and kept the arms of the king.

For the other Companions steeds were furnished according to their stature; and Frodo and Samwise rode at Aragorn's side, and Gandalf rode upon Shadowfax, and Pippin rode with the knights of Gondor; and Legolas and Gimli as ever rode together upon Arod.

In that riding went also Queen Arwen, and Celeborn and Galadriel with their folk, and Elrond and his sons; and the princes of Dol Amroth and of Ithilien, and many captains and knights. Never had any king of the Mark such company upon the road as went with Théoden Thengel's son to the land of his home.

Without haste and at peace they passed into Anórien, and they came to the Grey Wood under Amon Dîn; and there they heard a sound as of drums beating in the hills, though no living thing could be seen. Then Aragorn let the trumpets be blown; and heralds cried:

'Behold, the King Elessar is come! The Forest of Drúadan he gives to Ghân-buri-ghân and to his folk, to be their own for ever; and hereafter let no man enter it without their leave!'

Then the drums rolled loudly, and were silent.

At length after fifteen days of journey the wain of King Théoden passed through the green fields of Rohan and came to Edoras; and there they all rested. The Golden Hall was arrayed with fair hangings and it was filled with light, and there was held the highest feast that it had known since the days of its building. For after three days the Men of the Mark prepared the funeral of Théoden; and he was laid in a house of stone with his arms and many other fair things that he had possessed, and over him was raised a great mound, covered with green turves of grass and of white evermind. And now there were eight mounds on the east-side of the Barrowfield.

Then the Riders of the King's House upon white horses rode round about the barrow and sang together a song of Théoden Thengel's son that Gléowine his minstrel made, and he made no other song after. The slow voices of the Riders stirred the hearts even of those who did not know the speech of that people; but the words of the song brought a light to the eyes of the folk of the Mark as they heard again afar the thunder of the hooves of the North and the voice of Eorl crying above the battle upon the Field of Celebrant; and the tale of the kings rolled on, and the horn of Helm was loud in the mountains, until the Darkness came and King Théoden arose and rode through the Shadow to the fire, and died in splendour, even as the Sun, returning beyond hope, gleamed upon Mindolluin in the morning.

> *Out of doubt, out of dark, to the day's rising*
> *he rode singing in the sun, sword unsheathing.*
> *Hope he rekindled, and in hope ended;*
> *over death, over dread, over doom lifted*
> *out of loss, out of life, unto long glory.*

But Merry stood at the foot of the green mound, and he wept, and when the song was ended he arose and cried:

'Théoden King, Théoden King! Farewell! As a father you were to me, for a little while. Farewell!'

When the burial was over and the weeping of women was stilled, and Théoden was left at last alone in his barrow, then folk gathered to the Golden Hall for the great feast and put away sorrow; for Théoden had lived to full years and ended in honour no less than the greatest of his sires. And when the time came that in the custom of the Mark they should drink to the memory of the kings, Éowyn Lady of Rohan came forth, golden as the sun and white as snow, and she bore a filled cup to Éomer.

Then a minstrel and loremaster stood up and named all the names of the Lords of the Mark in their order: Eorl the Young; and Brego builder of the Hall; and Aldor brother of Baldor the hapless; and Fréa, and Fréawine, and Goldwine, and Déor, and Gram; and Helm who lay hid in Helm's Deep when the Mark was overrun; and so ended the nine mounds of the west-side, for in that time the line was broken, and after came the mounds of the east-side: Fréalaf, Helm's sister-son, and Léofa, and Walda, and Folca, and Folcwine, and Fengel, and Thengel, and Théoden the latest. And when Théoden was named Éomer drained the cup. Then Éowyn bade those that served to fill the cups, and all there assembled rose and drank to the new king, crying: 'Hail, Éomer, King of the Mark!'

At the last when the feast drew to an end Éomer arose and said: 'Now this is the funeral feast of Théoden the King; but I will speak ere we go of tidings of joy, for he would not grudge that I should do so, since he was ever a father to Éowyn my sister. Hear then all my guests, fair folk of many realms, such as have never before been gathered in this hall! Faramir, Steward of Gondor, and Prince of Ithilien, asks that Éowyn Lady of Rohan should be his wife, and she grants it full willing. Therefore they shall be trothplighted before you all.'

And Faramir and Éowyn stood forth and set hand in hand; and all there drank to them and were glad. 'Thus,' said Éomer, 'is the friendship of the Mark and of Gondor bound with a new bond, and the more do I rejoice.'

'No niggard are you, Éomer,' said Aragorn, 'to give thus to Gondor the fairest thing in your realm!'

Then Éowyn looked in the eyes of Aragorn, and she said: 'Wish me joy, my liege-lord and healer!'

And he answered: 'I have wished thee joy ever since first I saw thee. It heals my heart to see thee now in bliss.'

When the feast was over, those who were to go took leave of King Éomer. Aragorn and his knights, and the people of Lórien and of Rivendell, made ready to ride; but Faramir and Imrahil remained at Edoras; and Arwen Evenstar remained also, and she said farewell to her brethren. None saw her last meeting with Elrond her father, for they went up into the hills and there spoke long together, and bitter was their parting that should endure beyond the ends of the world.

At the last before the guests set out Éomer and Éowyn came to Merry, and they said: 'Farewell now, Meriadoc of the Shire and Holdwine of the Mark! Ride to good fortune, and ride back soon to our welcome!'

And Éomer said: 'Kings of old would have laden you with gifts that a wain could not bear for your deeds upon the fields of Mundburg; and yet you will take naught, you say, but the arms that were given to you. This I suffer, for indeed I have no gift that is worthy; but my sister begs you to receive this small thing, as a memorial of Dernhelm and of the horns of the Mark at the coming of the morning.'

Then Éowyn gave to Merry an ancient horn, small but cunningly wrought all of fair silver with a baldric of green; and wrights had engraven upon it swift horsemen riding in a line that wound about it from the tip to the mouth; and there were set runes of great virtue.

'This is an heirloom of our house,' said Éowyn. 'It was

made by the Dwarves, and came from the hoard of Scatha the Worm. Eorl the Young brought it from the North. He that blows it at need shall set fear in the hearts of his enemies and joy in the hearts of his friends, and they shall hear him and come to him.'

Then Merry took the horn, for it could not be refused, and he kissed Éowyn's hand; and they embraced him, and so they parted for that time.

Now the guests were ready, and they drank the stirrup-cup, and with great praise and friendship they departed, and came at length to Helm's Deep, and there they rested two days. Then Legolas repaid his promise to Gimli and went with him to the Glittering Caves; and when they returned he was silent, and would say only that Gimli alone could find fit words to speak of them. 'And never before has a Dwarf claimed a victory over an Elf in a contest of words,' said he. 'Now therefore let us go to Fangorn and set the score right!'

From Deeping-coomb they rode to Isengard, and saw how the Ents had busied themselves. All the stone-circle had been thrown down and removed, and the land within was made into a garden filled with orchards and trees, and a stream ran through it; but in the midst of all there was a lake of clear water, and out of it the Tower of Orthanc rose still, tall and impregnable, and its black rock was mirrored in the pool.

For a while the travellers sat where once the old gates of Isengard had stood, and there were now two tall trees like sentinels at the beginning of a green-bordered path that ran towards Orthanc; and they looked in wonder at the work that had been done, but no living thing could they see far or near. But presently they heard a voice calling *hoom-hom*, *hoom-hom*; and there came Treebeard striding down the path to greet them with Quickbeam at his side.

'Welcome to the Treegarth of Orthanc!' he said. 'I knew that you were coming, but I was at work up the valley; there is much still to be done. But you have not been idle either away in the south and the east, I hear; and all that I hear is good, very good.' Then Treebeard praised all their deeds, of which he seemed to have full knowledge; and at last he stopped and looked long at Gandalf.

'Well, come now!' he said. 'You have proved mightiest, and all your labours have gone well. Where now would you be going? And why do you come here?'

'To see how your work goes, my friend,' said Gandalf, 'and to thank you for your aid in all that has been achieved.'

'*Hoom*, well, that is fair enough,' said Treebeard; 'for to be sure Ents have played their part. And not only in dealing with that, *hoom*, that accursed tree-slayer that dwelt here. For there was a great inrush of those, *burárum*, those evileyed-blackhanded-bowlegged-flinthearted-clawfingered-foulbellied-bloodthirsty, *morimaite-sincahonda*, *hoom*, well, since you are hasty folk and their full name is as long as years of torment, those vermin of orcs; and they came over the River and down from the North and all round the wood of Laurelindórenan, which they could not get into, thanks to the Great ones who are here.' He bowed to the Lord and Lady of Lórien.

'And these same foul creatures were more than surprised to meet us out on the Wold, for they had not heard of us before; though that might be said also of better folk. And not many will remember us, for not many escaped us alive, and the River had most of those. But it was well for you, for if they had not met us, then the king of the grassland would not have ridden far, and if he had there would have been no home to return to.'

'We know it well,' said Aragorn, 'and never shall it be forgotten in Minas Tirith or in Edoras.'

'*Never* is too long a word even for me,' said Treebeard. 'Not while your kingdoms last, you mean; but they will have to last long indeed to seem long to Ents.'

'The New Age begins,' said Gandalf, 'and in this age it may well prove that the kingdoms of Men shall outlast you, Fangorn my friend. But now come tell me: what of the task that I set you? How is Saruman? Is he not weary of Orthanc yet? For I do not suppose that he will think you have improved the view from his windows.'

Treebeard gave Gandalf a long look, almost a cunning look, Merry thought. 'Ah!' he said. 'I thought you would come to that. Weary of Orthanc? Very weary at last; but not so weary of his tower as he was weary of my voice. *Hoom!* I gave him some long tales, or at least what might be thought long in your speech.'

'Then why did he stay to listen? Did you go into Orthanc?' asked Gandalf.

'*Hoom*, no, not into Orthanc!' said Treebeard. 'But he came to his window and listened, because he could not get news in any other way, and though he hated the news, he was greedy to have it; and I saw that he heard it all. But I added a great many things to the news that it was good for him to think of. He grew very weary. He always was hasty. That was his ruin.'

'I observe, my good Fangorn,' said Gandalf, 'that with great care you say *dwelt, was, grew*. What about *is*? Is he dead?'

'No, not dead, so far as I know,' said Treebeard. 'But he is gone. Yes, he is gone seven days. I let him go. There was little left of him when he crawled out, and as for that worm-creature of his, he was like a pale shadow. Now do not tell me, Gandalf, that I promised to keep him safe; for I know it. But things have changed since then. And I kept him until he was safe, safe from doing any more harm. You should know that above all I hate the caging of live things, and I will not keep even such creatures as these caged beyond great need. A snake without fangs may crawl where he will.'

'You may be right,' said Gandalf; 'but this snake had still one tooth left, I think. He had the poison of his voice, and I guess that he persuaded you, even you Treebeard, knowing the soft spot in your heart. Well, he is gone, and there is no more to be said. But the Tower of Orthanc now goes back to the King, to whom it belongs. Though maybe he will not need it.'

'That will be seen later,' said Aragorn. 'But I will give to Ents all this valley to do with as they will, so long as they keep a watch upon Orthanc and see that none enter it without my leave.'

'It is locked,' said Treebeard. 'I made Saruman lock it and give me the keys. Quickbeam has them.'

Quickbeam bowed like a tree bending in the wind and handed to Aragorn two great black keys of intricate shape, joined by a ring of steel. 'Now I thank you once more,' said Aragorn, 'and I bid you farewell. May your forest grow again in peace. When this valley is filled there is room and to spare west of the mountains, where once you walked long ago.'

Treebeard's face became sad. 'Forests may grow,' he said. 'Woods may spread. But not Ents. There are no Entings.'

'Yet maybe there is now more hope in your search,' said Aragorn. 'Lands will lie open to you eastward that have long been closed.'

But Treebeard shook his head and said: 'It is far to go. And there are too many Men there in these days. But I am forgetting my manners! Will you stay here and rest a while? And maybe there are some that would be pleased to pass through Fangorn Forest and so shorten their road home?' He looked at Celeborn and Galadriel.

But all save Legolas said that they must now take their leave and depart either south or west. 'Come, Gimli!' said Legolas. 'Now by Fangorn's leave I will visit the deep places of the Entwood and see such trees as are nowhere else to be found in Middle-earth. You shall come with me and keep your word; and thus we will journey on together to our own lands in Mirkwood and beyond.' To this Gimli agreed, though with no great delight, it seemed.

'Here then at last comes the ending of the Fellowship of the Ring,' said Aragorn. 'Yet I hope that ere long you will return to my land with the help that you promised.'

'We will come, if our own lords allow it,' said Gimli. 'Well, farewell, my hobbits! You should come safe to your own homes now, and I shall not be kept awake for fear of your peril. We will send word when we may, and some of us may yet meet at times; but I fear that we shall not all be gathered together ever again.'

Then Treebeard said farewell to each of them in turn, and he bowed three times slowly and with great reverence to Celeborn and Galadriel. 'It is long, long since we met by stock or by stone, *A vanimar, vanimálion nostari!*' he said. 'It is sad that we should meet only thus at the ending. For the world is changing: I feel it in the water, I feel it in the earth, and I smell it in the air. I do not think we shall meet again.'

And Celeborn said: 'I do not know, Eldest.' But Galadriel said: 'Not in Middle-earth, nor until the lands that lie under the wave are lifted up again. Then in the willow-meads of Tasarinan we may meet in the Spring. Farewell!'

Last of all Merry and Pippin said good-bye to the old Ent, and he grew gayer as he looked at them. 'Well, my merry folk,' he said, 'will you drink another draught with me before you go?'

'Indeed we will,' they said, and he took them aside into the shade of one of the trees, and there they saw that a great stone jar had been set. And Treebeard filled three bowls, and they drank; and they saw his strange eyes looking at them over the rim of his bowl. 'Take care, take care!' he said. 'For you have already grown since I saw you last.' And they laughed and drained their bowls.

'Well, good-bye!' he said. 'And don't forget that if you hear any news of the Entwives in your land, you will send word to me.' Then he waved his great hands to all the company and went off into the trees.

The travellers now rode with more speed, and they made their way towards the Gap of Rohan; and Aragorn took leave of them at last close to that very place where Pippin had looked into the Stone of Orthanc. The Hobbits were grieved at this parting; for Aragorn had never failed them and he had been their guide through many perils.

'I wish we could have a Stone that we could see all our friends in,' said Pippin, 'and that we could speak to them from far away!'

'Only one now remains that you could use,' answered Aragorn; 'for you would not wish to see what the Stone of Minas Tirith would show you. But the Palantír of Orthanc the King will keep, to see what is passing in his realm, and what his servants are doing. For do not forget, Peregrin Took, that you are a knight of Gondor, and I do not release you from your service. You are going now on leave, but I may recall you. And remember, dear friends of the Shire, that my realm lies also in the North, and I shall come there one day.'

Then Aragorn took leave of Celeborn and Galadriel; and the Lady said to him: 'Elfstone, through darkness you have come to your hope, and have now all your desire. Use well the days!'

But Celeborn said: 'Kinsman, farewell! May your doom be other than mine, and your treasure remain with you to the end!'

With that they parted, and it was then the time of sunset; and when after a while they turned and looked back, they saw the King of the West sitting upon his horse with his knights about him; and the falling Sun shone upon them and made all their harness to gleam like red gold, and the white mantle of Aragorn was turned to a flame. Then Aragorn took the green stone and held it up, and there came a green fire from his hand.

Soon the dwindling company, following the Isen, turned west and rode through the Gap into the waste lands beyond, and then they turned northwards, and passed over the borders of Dunland. The Dunlendings fled and hid themselves, for they were afraid of Elvish folk, though few indeed ever came to their country; but the travellers did not heed them, for they were still a great company and were well provided with all that they needed; and they went on their way at their leisure, setting up their tents when they would.

On the sixth day since their parting from the King they journeyed through a wood climbing down from the hills at the feet of the Misty Mountains that now marched on their right hand. As they came out again into the open country at sundown they overtook an old man leaning on a staff, and he was clothed in rags of grey or dirty white, and at his heels went another beggar, slouching and whining.

'Well Saruman!' said Gandalf. 'Where are you going?'

'What is that to you?' he answered. 'Will you still order my goings, and are you not content with my ruin?'

'You know the answers,' said Gandalf: 'no and no. But in any case the time of my labours now draws to an end. The King has taken on the burden. If you had waited at Orthanc, you would have seen him, and he would have shown you wisdom and mercy.'

'Then all the more reason to have left sooner,' said Saruman; 'for I desire neither of him. Indeed if you wish for an answer to your first question, I am seeking a way out of his realm.'

'Then once more you are going the wrong way,' said Gandalf, 'and I see no hope in your journey. But will you scorn our help? For we offer it to you.'

'To me?' said Saruman. 'Nay, pray do not smile at me! I prefer your frowns. And as for the Lady here, I do not trust her: she always hated me, and schemed for your part. I do not doubt that she has brought you this way to have the pleasure of gloating over my poverty. Had I been warned of your pursuit, I would have denied you the pleasure.'

'Saruman,' said Galadriel, 'we have other errands and other cares that seem to us more urgent than hunting for you. Say rather that you are overtaken by good fortune; for now you have a last chance.'

'If it be truly the last, I am glad,' said Saruman; 'for I shall be spared the trouble of refusing it again. All my hopes are ruined, but I would not share yours. If you have any.'

For a moment his eyes kindled. 'Go!' he said. 'I did not spend long study on these matters for naught. You have

doomed yourselves, and you know it. And it will afford me
some comfort as I wander to think that you pulled down
your own house when you destroyed mine. And now, what
ship will bear you back across so wide a sea?' he mocked. 'It
will be a grey ship, and full of ghosts.' He laughed, but his
voice was cracked and hideous.

'Get up, you idiot!' he shouted to the other beggar, who
had sat down on the ground; and he struck him with his
staff. 'Turn about! If these fine folk are going our way, then
we will take another. Get on, or I'll give you no crust for
your supper!'

The beggar turned and slouched past whimpering: 'Poor
old Gríma! Poor old Gríma! Always beaten and cursed. How
I hate him! I wish I could leave him!'

'Then leave him!' said Gandalf.

But Wormtongue only shot a glance of his bleared eyes full
of terror at Gandalf, and then shuffled quickly past behind
Saruman. As the wretched pair passed by the company they
came to the hobbits, and Saruman stopped and stared at
them; but they looked at him with pity.

'So you have come to gloat too, have you, my urchins?'
he said. 'You don't care what a beggar lacks, do you? For
you have all you want, food and fine clothes, and the best
weed for your pipes. Oh yes, I know! I know where it comes
from. You would not give a pipeful to a beggar, would
you?'

'I would, if I had any,' said Frodo.

'You can have what I have got left,' said Merry, 'if you
will wait a moment.' He got down and searched in the bag
at his saddle. Then he handed to Saruman a leather pouch.
'Take what there is,' he said. 'You are welcome to it; it came
from the flotsam of Isengard.'

'Mine, mine, yes and dearly bought!' cried Saruman,
clutching at the pouch. 'This is only a repayment in token;
for you took more, I'll be bound. Still, a beggar must be
grateful, if a thief returns him even a morsel of his own. Well,
it will serve you right when you come home, if you find

things less good in the Southfarthing than you would like. Long may your land be short of leaf!'

'Thank you!' said Merry. 'In that case I will have my pouch back, which is not yours and has journeyed far with me. Wrap the weed in a rag of your own.'

'One thief deserves another,' said Saruman, and turned his back on Merry, and kicked Wormtongue, and went away towards the wood.

'Well, I like that!' said Pippin. 'Thief indeed! What of our claim for waylaying, wounding, and orc-dragging us through Rohan?'

'Ah!' said Sam. 'And *bought* he said. How, I wonder? And I didn't like the sound of what he said about the Southfarthing. It's time we got back.'

'I'm sure it is,' said Frodo. 'But we can't go any quicker, if we are to see Bilbo. I am going to Rivendell first, whatever happens.'

'Yes, I think you had better do that,' said Gandalf. 'But alas for Saruman! I fear nothing more can be made of him. He has withered altogether. All the same, I am not sure that Treebeard is right: I fancy he could do some mischief still in a small mean way.'

Next day they went on into northern Dunland, where no men now dwelt, though it was a green and pleasant country. September came in with golden days and silver nights, and they rode at ease until they reached the Swanfleet river, and found the old ford, east of the falls where it went down suddenly into the lowlands. Far to the west in a haze lay the meres and eyots through which it wound its way to the Greyflood: there countless swans housed in a land of reeds.

So they passed into Eregion, and at last a fair morning dawned, shimmering above gleaming mists; and looking from their camp on a low hill the travellers saw away in the east the Sun catching three peaks that thrust up into the sky through floating clouds: Caradhras, Celebdil, and Fanuidhol. They were near to the Gates of Moria.

Here now for seven days they tarried, for the time was at hand for another parting which they were loth to make. Soon Celeborn and Galadriel and their folk would turn eastward, and so pass by the Redhorn Gate and down the Dimrill Stair to the Silverlode and to their own country. They had journeyed thus far by the west-ways, for they had much to speak of with Elrond and with Gandalf, and here they lingered still in converse with their friends. Often long after the hobbits were wrapped in sleep they would sit together under the stars, recalling the ages that were gone and all their joys and labours in the world, or holding council, concerning the days to come. If any wanderer had chanced to pass, little would he have seen or heard, and it would have seemed to him only that he saw grey figures, carved in stone, memorials of forgotten things now lost in unpeopled lands. For they did not move or speak with mouth, looking from mind to mind; and only their shining eyes stirred and kindled as their thoughts went to and fro.

But at length all was said, and they parted again for a while, until it was time for the Three Rings to pass away. Quickly fading into the stones and the shadows the grey-cloaked people of Lórien rode towards the mountains; and those who were going to Rivendell sat on the hill and watched, until there came out of the gathering mist a flash; and then they saw no more. Frodo knew that Galadriel had held aloft her ring in token of farewell.

Sam turned away and sighed: 'I wish I was going back to Lórien!'

At last one evening they came over the high moors, suddenly as to travellers it always seemed, to the brink of the deep valley of Rivendell and saw far below the lamps shining in Elrond's house. And they went down and crossed the bridge and came to the doors, and all the house was filled with light and song for joy at Elrond's homecoming.

First of all, before they had eaten or washed or even shed their cloaks, the hobbits went in search of Bilbo. They found him all alone in his little room. It was littered with papers and pens and pencils; but Bilbo was sitting in a chair before a small bright fire. He looked very old, but peaceful, and sleepy.

He opened his eyes and looked up as they came in. 'Hullo, hullo!' he said. 'So you've come back? And tomorrow's my birthday, too. How clever of you! Do you know, I shall be one hundred and twenty-nine? And in one year more, if I am spared, I shall equal the Old Took. I should like to beat him; but we shall see.'

After the celebration of Bilbo's birthday the four hobbits stayed in Rivendell for some days, and they sat much with their old friend, who spent most of his time now in his room, except at meals. For these he was still very punctual as a rule, and he seldom failed to wake up in time for them. Sitting round the fire they told him in turn all that they could remember of their journeys and adventures. At first he pretended to take some notes; but he often fell asleep; and when he woke he would say: 'How splendid! How wonderful! But where were we?' Then they went on with the story from the point where he had begun to nod.

The only part that seemed really to rouse him and hold his attention was the account of the crowning and marriage of Aragorn. 'I was invited to the wedding, of course,' he said. 'And I have waited for it long enough. But somehow, when it came to it, I found I had so much to do here; and packing is such a bother.'

When nearly a fortnight had passed Frodo looked out of his window and saw that there had been a frost in the night, and the cobwebs were like white nets. Then suddenly he knew that he must go, and say good-bye to Bilbo. The weather was still calm and fair, after one of the most lovely summers that people could remember; but October had come, and it must break soon and begin to rain and blow again. And there was still a very long way to go. Yet it was not really the thought of the weather that stirred him. He had a feeling that it was

time he went back to the Shire. Sam shared it. Only the night
before he had said:

'Well, Mr. Frodo, we've been far and seen a deal, and yet
I don't think we've found a better place than this. There's
something of everything here, if you understand me: the Shire
and the Golden Wood and Gondor and kings' houses and
inns and meadows and mountains all mixed. And yet, somehow, I feel we ought to be going soon. I'm worried about
my gaffer, to tell you the truth.'

'Yes, something of everything, Sam, except the Sea,' Frodo
had answered; and he repeated it now to himself: 'Except
the Sea.'

That day Frodo spoke to Elrond, and it was agreed that
they should leave the next morning. To their delight Gandalf
said: 'I think I shall come too. At least as far as Bree. I want
to see Butterbur.'

In the evening they went to say good-bye to Bilbo. 'Well,
if you must go, you must,' he said. 'I am sorry. I shall miss
you. It is nice just to know that you are about the place. But
I am getting very sleepy.' Then he gave Frodo his mithril-coat
and Sting, forgetting that he had already done so; and he
gave him also three books of lore that he had made at various
times, written in his spidery hand, and labelled on their red
backs: *Translations from the Elvish, by B.B.*

To Sam he gave a little bag of gold. 'Almost the last drop
of the Smaug vintage,' he said. 'May come in useful, if you
think of getting married, Sam.' Sam blushed.

'I have nothing much to give to you young fellows,' he
said to Merry and Pippin, 'except good advice.' And when
he had given them a fair sample of this, he added a last item
in Shire-fashion: 'Don't let your heads get too big for your
hats! But if you don't finish growing up soon, you are going
to find hats and clothes expensive.'

'But if you want to beat the Old Took,' said Pippin, 'I
don't see why we shouldn't try and beat the Bullroarer.'

Bilbo laughed, and he produced out of a pocket two beautiful pipes with pearl mouth-pieces and bound with fine-

wrought silver. 'Think of me when you smoke them!' he said. 'The Elves made them for me, but I don't smoke now.' And then suddenly he nodded and went to sleep for a little; and when he woke up again he said: 'Now where were we? Yes, of course, giving presents. Which reminds me: what's become of my ring, Frodo, that you took away?'

'I have lost it, Bilbo dear,' said Frodo. 'I got rid of it, you know.'

'What a pity!' said Bilbo. 'I should have liked to see it again. But no, how silly of me! That's what you went for, wasn't it: to get rid of it? But it is all so confusing, for such a lot of other things seem to have got mixed up with it: Aragorn's affairs, and the White Council, and Gondor, and the Horsemen, and Southrons, and oliphaunts – did you really see one, Sam? – and caves and towers and golden trees, and goodness knows what besides.

'I evidently came back by much too straight a road from my trip. I think Gandalf might have shown me round a bit. But then the auction would have been over before I got back, and I should have had even more trouble than I did. Anyway it's too late now; and really I think it's much more comfortable to sit here and hear about it all. The fire's very cosy here, and the food's *very* good, and there are Elves when you want them. What more could one want?

> *The Road goes ever on and on*
>   *Out from the door where it began.*
> *Now far ahead the Road has gone,*
>   *Let others follow it who can!*
> *Let them a journey new begin,*
>   *But I at last with weary feet*
> *Will turn towards the lighted inn,*
>   *My evening-rest and sleep to meet.'*

And as Bilbo murmured the last words his head dropped on his chest and he slept soundly.

*   *   *

The evening deepened in the room, and the firelight burned brighter; and they looked at Bilbo as he slept and saw that his face was smiling. For some time they sat in silence; and then Sam looking round at the room and the shadows flickering on the walls, said softly:

'I don't think, Mr. Frodo, that he's done much writing while we've been away. He won't ever write our story now.'

At that Bilbo opened an eye, almost as if he had heard. Then he roused himself. 'You see, I am getting so sleepy,' he said. 'And when I have time to write, I only really like writing poetry. I wonder, Frodo my dear fellow, if you would very much mind tidying things up a bit before you go? Collect all my notes and papers, and my diary too, and take them with you, if you will. You see, I haven't much time for the selection and the arrangement and all that. Get Sam to help, and when you've knocked things into shape, come back, and I'll run over it. I won't be too critical.'

'Of course I'll do it!' said Frodo. 'And of course I'll come back soon: it won't be dangerous any more. There is a real king now, and he will soon put the roads in order.'

'Thank you, my dear fellow!' said Bilbo. 'That really is a very great relief to my mind.' And with that he fell asleep again.

The next day Gandalf and the hobbits took leave of Bilbo in his room, for it was cold out of doors; and then they said farewell to Elrond and all his household.

As Frodo stood upon the threshold, Elrond wished him a fair journey, and blessed him, and he said:

'I think, Frodo, that maybe you will not need to come back, unless you come very soon. For about this time of the year, when the leaves are gold before they fall, look for Bilbo in the woods of the Shire. I shall be with him.'

These words no one else heard, and Frodo kept them to himself.

CHAPTER VII

HOMEWARD BOUND

At last the hobbits had their faces turned towards home. They were eager now to see the Shire again; but at first they rode only slowly, for Frodo had been ill at ease. When they came to the Ford of Bruinen, he had halted, and seemed loth to ride into the stream; and they noted that for a while his eyes appeared not to see them or things about him. All that day he was silent. It was the sixth of October.

'Are you in pain, Frodo?' said Gandalf quietly as he rode by Frodo's side.

'Well, yes I am,' said Frodo. 'It is my shoulder. The wound aches, and the memory of darkness is heavy on me. It was a year ago today.'

'Alas! there are some wounds that cannot be wholly cured,' said Gandalf.

'I fear it may be so with mine,' said Frodo. 'There is no real going back. Though I may come to the Shire, it will not seem the same; for I shall not be the same. I am wounded with knife, sting, and tooth, and a long burden. Where shall I find rest?'

Gandalf did not answer.

By the end of the next day the pain and unease had passed, and Frodo was merry again, as merry as if he did not remember the blackness of the day before. After that the journey went well, and the days went quickly by; for they rode at leisure, and often they lingered in the fair woodlands where the leaves were red and yellow in the autumn sun. At length they came to Weathertop; and it was then drawing towards evening and the shadow of the hill lay dark on the road. Then Frodo begged them to hasten, and he would not look towards the hill, but rode through its shadow with head bowed and cloak drawn close about him. That night the weather changed, and a wind came from the West laden with rain, and it blew loud and chill, and the yellow leaves whirled like birds in the air. When they came to the Chetwood already the boughs were almost bare, and a great curtain of rain veiled Bree Hill from their sight.

So it was that near the end of a wild and wet evening in the last days of October the five travellers rode up the climbing road and came to the South-gate of Bree. It was locked fast; and the rain blew in their faces, and in the darkening sky low clouds went hurrying by, and their hearts sank a little, for they had expected more welcome.

When they had called many times, at last the Gate-keeper came out, and they saw that he carried a great cudgel. He looked at them with fear and suspicion; but when he saw that Gandalf was there, and that his companions were hobbits, in spite of their strange gear, then he brightened and wished them welcome.

'Come in!' he said, unlocking the gate. 'We won't stay for news out here in the cold and the wet, a ruffianly evening. But old Barley will no doubt give you a welcome at *The Pony*, and there you'll hear all there is to hear.'

'And there you'll hear later all that we say, and more,' laughed Gandalf. 'How is Harry?'

The Gate-keeper scowled. 'Gone,' he said. 'But you'd best ask Barliman. Good evening!'

'Good evening to you!' they said, and passed through; and then they noticed that behind the hedge at the road-side a long low hut had been built, and a number of men had come out and were staring at them over the fence. When they came to Bill Ferny's house they saw that the hedge there was tattered and unkempt, and the windows were all boarded up.

'Do you think you killed him with that apple, Sam?' said Pippin.

'I'm not so hopeful, Mr. Pippin,' said Sam. 'But I'd like

to know what became of that poor pony. He's been on my mind many a time, and the wolves howling and all.'

At last they came to *The Prancing Pony*, and that at least looked outwardly unchanged; and there were lights behind the red curtains in the lower windows. They rang the bell, and Nob came to the door, and opened it a crack and peeped through; and when he saw them standing under the lamp he gave a cry of surprise.

'Mr. Butterbur! Master!' he shouted. 'They've come back!'

'Oh have they? I'll learn them,' came Butterbur's voice, and out he came with a rush, and he had a club in his hand. But when he saw who they were he stopped short, and the black scowl on his face changed to wonder and delight.

'Nob, you woolly-pated ninny!' he cried. 'Can't you give old friends their names? You shouldn't go scaring me like that, with times as they are. Well, well! And where have you come from? I never expected to see any of you folk again, and that's a fact: going off into the Wild with that Strider, and all those Black Men about. But I'm right glad to see you, and none more than Gandalf. Come in! Come in! The same rooms as before? They're free. Indeed most rooms are empty these days, as I'll not hide from you, for you'll find it out soon enough. And I'll see what can be done about supper, as soon as may be; but I'm short-handed at present. Hey, Nob you slowcoach! Tell Bob! Ah, but there I'm forgetting, Bob's gone: goes home to his folk at nightfall now. Well, take the guests' ponies to the stables, Nob! And you'll be taking your horse to his stable yourself, Gandalf, I don't doubt. A fine beast, as I said when I first set eyes on him. Well, come in! Make yourselves at home!'

Mr. Butterbur had at any rate not changed his manner of talking, and still seemed to live in his old breathless bustle. And yet there was hardly anybody about, and all was quiet; from the Common Room there came a low murmur of no more than two or three voices. And seen closer in the light of two candles that he lit and carried before them the land-lord's face looked rather wrinkled and careworn.

He led them down the passage to the parlour that they had used on that strange night more than a year ago; and they followed him, a little disquieted, for it seemed plain to them that old Barliman was putting a brave face on some trouble. Things were not what they had been. But they said nothing, and waited.

As they expected Mr. Butterbur came to the parlour after supper to see if all had been to their liking. As indeed it had: no change for the worse had yet come upon the beer or the victuals at *The Pony*, at any rate. 'Now I won't make so bold as to suggest you should come to the Common Room tonight,' said Butterbur. 'You'll be tired; and there isn't many folk there this evening, anyway. But if you could spare me half an hour before you go to your beds, I would dearly like to have some talk with you, quiet-like by ourselves.'

'That is just what we should like, too,' said Gandalf. 'We are not tired. We have been taking things easy. We were wet, cold and hungry, but all that you have cured. Come, sit down! And if you have any pipe-weed, we'll bless you.'

'Well, if you'd called for anything else, I'd have been hap-pier,' said Butterbur. 'That's just a thing that we're short of, seeing how we've only got what we grow ourselves, and that's not enough. There's none to be had from the Shire these days. But I'll do what I can.'

When he came back he brought them enough to last them for a day or two, a wad of uncut leaf. 'Southlinch,' he said, 'and the best we have; but not the match of Southfarthing, as I've always said, though I'm all for Bree in most matters, begging your pardon.'

They put him in a large chair by the wood-fire, and Gan-dalf sat on the other side of the hearth, and the hobbits in low chairs between them; and then they talked for many times half an hour, and exchanged all such news as Mr. Butterbur wished to hear or give. Most of the things which they had to tell were a mere wonder and bewilderment to their host, and far beyond his vision; and they brought forth few comments other than: 'You don't say,' often repeated in defiance of the evidence of Mr. Butterbur's own ears. 'You don't say, Mr. Baggins, or is it Mr. Underhill? I'm getting so mixed up. You don't say, Master Gandalf! Well I never! Who'd have thought it in our times!'

But he did say much on his own account. Things were far from well, he would say. Business was not even fair, it was downright bad. 'No one comes nigh Bree now from Outside,' he said. 'And the inside folks, they stay at home mostly and keep their doors barred. It all comes of those newcomers and gangrels that began coming up the Greenway last year, as you may remember; but more came later. Some were just poor bodies running away from trouble; but most were bad men, full o' thievery and mischief. And there was trouble right here in Bree, bad trouble. Why, we had a real set-to, and there were some folk killed, killed dead! If you'll believe me.'

'I will indeed,' said Gandalf. 'How many?'

'Three and two,' said Butterbur, referring to the big folk and the little. 'There was poor Mat Heathertoes, and Rowlie Appledore, and little Tom Pickthorn from over the Hill; and Willie Banks from up-away, and one of the Underhills from Staddle: all good fellows, and they're missed. And Harry Goatleaf that used to be on the West-gate, and that Bill Ferny, they came in on the strangers' side, and they've gone off with them; and it's my belief they let them in. On the night of the fight, I mean. And that was after we showed them the gates and pushed them out: before the year's end, that was; and the fight was early in the New Year, after the heavy snow we had.

'And now they're gone for robbers and live outside, hiding in the woods beyond Archet, and out in the wilds north-away. It's like a bit of the bad old times tales tell of, I say. It isn't safe on the road and nobody goes far, and folk lock up early. We have to keep watchers all round the fence and put a lot of men on the gates at nights.'

'Well, no one troubled us,' said Pippin, 'and we came along slowly, and kept no watch. We thought we'd left all trouble behind us.'

'Ah, that you haven't, Master, more's the pity,' said Butterbur. 'But it's no wonder they left you alone. They wouldn't go for armed folk, with swords and helmets and shields and all. Make them think twice, that would. And I must say it put me aback a bit when I saw you.'

Then the hobbits suddenly realized that people had looked at them with amazement not out of surprise at their return so much as in wonder at their gear. They themselves had become so used to warfare and to riding in well-arrayed companies that they had quite forgotten that the bright mail peeping from under their cloaks, and the helms of Gondor and the Mark, and the fair devices on their shields, would seem outlandish in their own country. And Gandalf, too, was now riding on his tall grey horse, all clad in white with a great mantle of blue and silver over all, and the long sword Glamdring at his side.

Gandalf laughed. 'Well, well,' he said, 'if they are afraid of just five of us, then we have met worse enemies on our travels. But at any rate they will give you peace at night while we stay.'

'How long will that be?' said Butterbur. 'I'll not deny we should be glad to have you about for a bit. You see, we're not used to such troubles; and the Rangers have all gone away, folk tell me. I don't think we've rightly understood till now what they did for us. For there's been worse than robbers about. Wolves were howling round the fences last winter. And there's dark shapes in the woods, dreadful things that it makes the blood run cold to think of. It's been very disturbing, if you understand me.'

'I expect it has,' said Gandalf. 'Nearly all lands have been disturbed these days, very disturbed. But cheer up, Barliman! You have been on the edge of very great troubles, and I am only glad to hear that you have not been deeper in. But better times are coming. Maybe, better than any you remember.

The Rangers have returned. We came back with them. And there is a king again, Barliman. He will soon be turning his mind this way.

'Then the Greenway will be opened again, and his messengers will come north, and there will be comings and goings, and the evil things will be driven out of the waste-lands. Indeed the waste in time will be waste no longer, and there will be people and fields where once there was wilderness.'

Mr. Butterbur shook his head. 'If there's a few decent respectable folk on the roads, that won't do no harm,' he said. 'But we don't want no more rabble and ruffians. And we don't want no outsiders at Bree, nor near Bree at all. We want to be let alone. I don't want a whole crowd o' strangers camping here and settling there and tearing up the wild country.'

'You will be let alone, Barliman,' said Gandalf. 'There is room enough for realms between Isen and Greyflood, or along the shore-lands south of the Brandywine, without any one living within many days' ride of Bree. And many folk used to dwell away north, a hundred miles or more from here, at the far end of the Greenway: on the North Downs or by Lake Evendim.'

'Up away by Deadmen's Dike?' said Butterbur, looking even more dubious. 'That's haunted land, they say. None but a robber would go there.'

'The Rangers go there,' said Gandalf. 'Deadmen's Dike, you say. So it has been called for long years; but its right name, Barliman, is Fornost Erain, Norbury of the Kings. And the King will come there again one day; and then you'll have some fair folk riding through.'

'Well, that sounds more hopeful, I'll allow,' said Butterbur. 'And it will be good for business, no doubt. So long as he lets Bree alone.'

'He will,' said Gandalf. 'He knows it and loves it.'

'Does he now?' said Butterbur looking puzzled. 'Though I'm sure I don't know why he should, sitting in his big chair up in his great castle, hundreds of miles away. And drinking wine out of a golden cup, I shouldn't wonder. What's *The Pony* to him, or mugs o' beer? Not but what my beer's good, Gandalf. It's been uncommon good, since you came in the autumn of last year and put a good word on it. And that's been a comfort in trouble, I will say.'

'Ah!' said Sam. 'But he says your beer is always good.'

'He says?'

'Of course he does. He's Strider. The chief of the Rangers. Haven't you got that into your head yet?'

It went in at last, and Butterbur's face was a study in wonder. The eyes in his broad face grew round, and his mouth opened wide, and he gasped. 'Strider!' he exclaimed when he got back his breath. 'Him with a crown and all and a golden cup! Well, what are we coming to?'

'Better times, for Bree at any rate,' said Gandalf.

'I hope so, I'm sure,' said Butterbur. 'Well, this has been the nicest chat I've had in a month of Mondays. And I'll not deny that I'll sleep easier tonight and with a lighter heart. You've given me a powerful lot to think over, but I'll put that off until tomorrow. I'm for bed, and I've no doubt you'll be glad of your beds too. Hey, Nob!' he called, going to the door. 'Nob, you slowcoach!'

'Nob!' he said to himself, slapping his forehead. 'Now what does that remind me of?'

'Not another letter you've forgotten, I hope, Mr. Butterbur?' said Merry.

'Now, now, Mr. Brandybuck, don't go reminding me of that! But there, you've broken my thought. Now where was I? Nob, stables, ah! that was it. I've something that belongs to you. If you recollect Bill Ferny and the horsethieving: his pony as you bought, well, it's here. Come back all of itself, it did. But where it had been to you know better than me. It was as shaggy as an old dog and as lean as a clothes-rail, but it was alive. Nob's looked after it.'

'What! My Bill?' cried Sam. 'Well, I was born lucky, whatever my gaffer may say. There's another wish come true!

Where is he?' Sam would not go to bed until he had visited Bill in his stable.

The travellers stayed in Bree all the next day, and Mr. Butterbur could not complain of his business next evening at any rate. Curiosity overcame all fears, and his house was crowded. For a while out of politeness the hobbits visited the Common Room in the evening and answered a good many questions. Bree memories being retentive, Frodo was asked many times if he had written his book.

'Not yet,' he answered. 'I am going home now to put my notes in order.' He promised to deal with the amazing events at Bree, and so give a bit of interest to a book that appeared likely to treat mostly of the remote and less important affairs 'away south'.

Then one of the younger folk called for a song. But at that a hush fell, and he was frowned down, and the call was not repeated. Evidently there was no wish for any uncanny events in the Common Room again.

No trouble by day, nor any sound by night, disturbed the peace of Bree while the travellers remained there; but the next morning they got up early, for as the weather was still rainy they wished to reach the Shire before night, and it was a long ride. The Bree folk were all out to see them off, and were in merrier mood than they had been for a year; and those who had not seen the strangers in all their gear before gaped with wonder at them: at Gandalf with his white beard, and the light that seemed to gleam from him, as if his blue mantle was only a cloud over sunshine; and at the four hobbits like riders upon errantry out of almost forgotten tales. Even those who had laughed at all the talk about the King began to think there might be some truth in it.

'Well, good luck on your road, and good luck to your homecoming!' said Mr. Butterbur. 'I should have warned you before that all's not well in the Shire neither, if what we hear is true. Funny goings on, they say. But one thing drives out another, and I was full of my own troubles. But if I may be so bold, you've come back changed from your travels, and you look now like folk as can deal with troubles out of hand. I don't doubt you'll soon set all to rights. Good luck to you! And the oftener you come back the better I'll be pleased.'

They wished him farewell and rode away, and passed through the West-gate and on towards the Shire. Bill the pony was with them, and as before he had a good deal of baggage, but he trotted along beside Sam and seemed well content.

'I wonder what old Barliman was hinting at,' said Frodo.

'I can guess some of it,' said Sam gloomily. 'What I saw in the Mirror: trees cut down and all, and my old gaffer turned out of the Row. I ought to have hurried back quicker.'

'And something's wrong with the Southfarthing evidently,' said Merry. 'There's a general shortage of pipe-weed.'

'Whatever it is,' said Pippin, 'Lotho will be at the bottom of it: you can be sure of that.'

'Deep in, but not at the bottom,' said Gandalf. 'You have forgotten Saruman. He began to take an interest in the Shire before Mordor did.'

'Well, we've got you with us,' said Merry, 'so things will soon be cleared up.'

'I am with you at present,' said Gandalf, 'but soon I shall not be. I am not coming to the Shire. You must settle its affairs yourselves; that is what you have been trained for. Do you not yet understand? My time is over: it is no longer my task to set things to rights, nor to help folk to do so. And as for you, my dear friends, you will need no help. You are grown up now. Grown indeed very high; among the great you are, and I have no longer any fear at all for any of you.

'But if you would know, I am turning aside soon. I am going to have a long talk with Bombadil: such a talk as I have not had in all my time. He is a moss-gatherer, and I have been a stone doomed to rolling. But my rolling days are ending, and now we shall have much to say to one another.'

★   ★   ★

In a little while they came to the point on the East Road where they had taken leave of Bombadil; and they hoped and half expected to see him standing there to greet them as they went by. But there was no sign of him; and there was a grey mist on the Barrow-downs southwards, and a deep veil over the Old Forest far away.

They halted and Frodo looked south wistfully. 'I should dearly like to see the old fellow again,' he said. 'I wonder how he is getting on?'

'As well as ever, you may be sure,' said Gandalf. 'Quite untroubled; and I should guess, not much interested in anything that we have done or seen, unless perhaps in our visits to the Ents. There may be a time later for you to go and see him. But if I were you, I should press on now for home, or you will not come to the Brandywine Bridge before the gates are locked.'

'But there aren't any gates,' said Merry, 'not on the Road; you know that quite well. There's the Buckland Gate, of course; but they'll let me through that at any time.'

'There weren't any gates, you mean,' said Gandalf. 'I think you will find some now. And you might have more trouble even at the Buckland Gate than you think. But you'll manage all right. Good-bye, dear friends! Not for the last time, not yet. Good-bye!'

He turned Shadowfax off the Road, and the great horse leaped the green dike that here ran beside it; and then at a cry from Gandalf he was gone, racing towards the Barrow-downs like a wind from the North.

'Well here we are, just the four of us that started out together,' said Merry. 'We have left all the rest behind, one after another. It seems almost like a dream that has slowly faded.'

'Not to me,' said Frodo. 'To me it feels more like falling asleep again.'

CHAPTER VIII

THE SCOURING OF THE SHIRE

It was after nightfall when, wet and tired, the travellers came at last to the Brandywine, and they found the way barred. At either end of the Bridge there was a great spiked gate; and on the further side of the river they could see that some new houses had been built: two-storeyed with narrow straight-sided windows, bare and dimly lit, all very gloomy and un-Shirelike.

They hammered on the outer gate and called, but there was at first no answer; and then to their surprise someone blew a horn, and the lights in the windows went out. A voice shouted in the dark:

'Who's that? Be off! You can't come in. Can't you read the notice: *No admittance between sundown and sunrise?*'

'Of course we can't read the notice in the dark,' Sam shouted back. 'And if hobbits of the Shire are to be kept out in the wet on a night like this, I'll tear down your notice when I find it.'

At that a window slammed, and a crowd of hobbits with lanterns poured out of the house on the left. They opened the further gate, and some came over the bridge. When they saw the travellers they seemed frightened.

'Come along!' said Merry, recognizing one of the hobbits. 'If you don't know me, Hob Hayward, you ought to. I am Merry Brandybuck, and I should like to know what all this is about, and what a Bucklander like you is doing here. You used to be on the Hay Gate.'

'Bless me! It's Master Merry, to be sure, and all dressed up for fighting!' said old Hob. 'Why, they said you was dead! Lost in the Old Forest by all accounts. I'm pleased to see you alive after all!'

'Then stop gaping at me through the bars, and open the gate!' said Merry.

'I'm sorry, Master Merry, but we have orders.'

'Whose orders?'

'The Chief's up at Bag End.'

'Chief? Chief? Do you mean Mr. Lotho?' said Frodo.

'I suppose so, Mr. Baggins; but we have to say just "the Chief" nowadays.'

'Do you indeed!' said Frodo. 'Well, I am glad he has dropped the Baggins at any rate. But it is evidently high time that the family dealt with him and put him in his place.'

A hush fell on the hobbits beyond the gate. 'It won't do no good talking that way,' said one. 'He'll get to hear of it. And if you make so much noise, you'll wake the Chief's Big Man.'

'We shall wake him up in a way that will surprise him,' said Merry. 'If you mean that your precious Chief has been hiring ruffians out of the wild, then we've not come back too soon.' He sprang from his pony, and seeing the notice in the light of the lanterns, he tore it down and threw it over the gate. The hobbits backed away and made no move to open it. 'Come on, Pippin!' said Merry. 'Two is enough.'

Merry and Pippin climbed the gate, and the hobbits fled. Another horn sounded. Out of the bigger house on the right a large heavy figure appeared against a light in the doorway.

'What's all this,' he snarled as he came forward. 'Gate-breaking? You clear out, or I'll break your filthy little necks!' Then he stopped, for he had caught the gleam of swords.

'Bill Ferny,' said Merry, 'if you don't open that gate in ten seconds, you'll regret it. I shall set steel to you, if you don't obey. And when you have opened the gates you will go through them and never return. You are a ruffian and a highway-robber.'

Bill Ferny flinched and shuffled to the gate and unlocked it. 'Give me the key!' said Merry. But the ruffian flung it at his head and then darted out into the darkness. As he passed the ponies one of them let fly with his heels and just caught him as he ran. He went off with a yelp into the night and was never heard of again.

'Neat work, Bill,' said Sam, meaning the pony.

'So much for your Big Man,' said Merry. 'We'll see the Chief later. In the meantime we want a lodging for the night, and as you seem to have pulled down the Bridge Inn and built this dismal place instead, you'll have to put us up.'

'I am sorry, Mr. Merry,' said Hob, 'but it isn't allowed.'

'What isn't allowed?'

'Taking in folk off-hand like, and eating extra food, and all that,' said Hob.

'What's the matter with the place?' said Merry. 'Has it been a bad year, or what? I thought it had been a fine summer and harvest.'

'Well no, the year's been good enough,' said Hob. 'We grows a lot of food, but we don't rightly know what becomes of it. It's all these "gatherers" and "sharers", I reckon, going round counting and measuring and taking off to storage. They do more gathering than sharing, and we never see most of the stuff again.'

'Oh come!' said Pippin yawning. 'This is all too tiresome for me tonight. We've got food in our bags. Just give us a room to lie down in. It'll be better than many places I have seen.'

The hobbits at the gate still seemed ill at ease, evidently some rule or other was being broken; but there was no gainsaying four such masterful travellers, all armed, and two of them uncommonly large and strong-looking. Frodo ordered the gates to be locked again. There was some sense at any rate in keeping a guard, while ruffians were still about. Then the four companions went into the hobbit guard-house and made themselves as comfortable as they could. It was a bare and ugly place, with a mean little grate that would not allow a good fire. In the upper rooms were little rows of hard beds, and on every wall there was a notice and a list of Rules.

Pippin tore them down. There was no beer and very little food, but with what the travellers brought and shared out they all made a fair meal; and Pippin broke Rule 4 by putting most of next day's allowance of wood on the fire.

'Well now, what about a smoke, while you tell us what has been happening in the Shire?' he said.

'There isn't no pipe-weed now,' said Hob; 'at least only for the Chief's men. All the stocks seem to have gone. We do hear that waggon-loads of it went away down the old road out of the Southfarthing, over Sarn Ford way. That would be the end o' last year, after you left. But it had been going away quietly before that, in a small way. That Lotho———'

'Now you shut up, Hob Hayward!' cried several of the others. 'You know talk o' that sort isn't allowed. The Chief will hear of it, and we'll all be in trouble.'

'He wouldn't hear naught, if some of you here weren't sneaks,' rejoined Hob hotly.

'All right, all right!' said Sam. 'That's quite enough. I don't want to hear no more. No welcome, no beer, no smoke, and a lot of rules and orc-talk instead. I hoped to have a rest, but I can see there's work and trouble ahead. Let's sleep and forget it till morning!'

The new 'Chief' evidently had means of getting news. It was a good forty miles from the Bridge to Bag End, but someone made the journey in a hurry. So Frodo and his friends soon discovered.

They had not made any definite plans, but had vaguely thought of going down to Crickhollow together first, and resting there a bit. But now, seeing what things were like, they decided to go straight to Hobbiton. So the next day they set out along the Road and jogged along steadily. The wind had dropped but the sky was grey. The land looked rather sad and forlorn; but it was after all the first of November and the fag-end of Autumn. Still there seemed an unusual amount of burning going on, and smoke rose from many points round about. A great cloud of it was going up far away in the direction of the Woody End.

As evening fell they were drawing near to Frogmorton, a village right on the Road, about twenty-two miles from the Bridge. There they meant to stay the night; *The Floating Log* at Frogmorton was a good inn. But as they came to the east end of the village they met a barrier with a large board saying NO ROAD; and behind it stood a large band of Shirriffs with staves in their hands and feathers in their caps, looking both important and rather scared.

'What's all this?' said Frodo, feeling inclined to laugh.

'This is what it is, Mr. Baggins,' said the leader of the Shirriffs, a two-feather hobbit: 'You're arrested for Gate-breaking, and Tearing up of Rules, and Assaulting Gate-keepers, and Trespassing, and Sleeping in Shire-buildings without Leave, and Bribing Guards with Food.'

'And what else?' said Frodo.

'That'll do to go on with,' said the Shirriff-leader.

'I can add some more, if you'd like it,' said Sam. 'Calling your Chief Names, Wishing to punch his Pimply Face, and Thinking you Shirriffs look a lot of Tom-fools.'

'There now, Mister, that'll do. It's the Chief's orders that you're to come along quiet. We're going to take you to Bywater and hand you over to the Chief's Men; and when he deals with your case you can have your say. But if you don't want to stay in the Lockholes any longer than you need, I should cut the say short, if I was you.'

To the discomfiture of the Shirriffs Frodo and his companions all roared with laughter. 'Don't be absurd!' said Frodo. 'I am going where I please, and in my own time. I happen to be going to Bag End on business, but if you insist on going too, well that is your affair.'

'Very well, Mr. Baggins,' said the leader, pushing the barrier aside. 'But don't forget I've arrested you.'

'I won't,' said Frodo. 'Never. But I may forgive you. Now I am not going any further today, so if you'll kindly escort me to *The Floating Log*, I'll be obliged.'

'I can't do that, Mr. Baggins. The inn's closed. There's a Shirriff-house at the far end of the village. I'll take you there.'

'All right,' said Frodo. 'Go on and we'll follow.'

Sam had been looking the Shirriffs up and down and had spotted one that he knew. 'Hey, come here Robin Smallburrow!' he called. 'I want a word with you.'

With a sheepish glance at his leader, who looked wrathful but did not dare to interfere, Shirriff Smallburrow fell back and walked beside Sam, who got down off his pony.

'Look here, Cock-robin!' said Sam. 'You're Hobbiton-bred and ought to have more sense, coming a-waylaying Mr. Frodo and all. And what's all this about the inn being closed?'

'They're all closed,' said Robin. 'The Chief doesn't hold with beer. Leastways that is how it started. But now I reckon it's his Men that has it all. And he doesn't hold with folk moving about; so if they will or they must, then they has to go to the Shirriff-house and explain their business.'

'You ought to be ashamed of yourself having anything to do with such nonsense,' said Sam. 'You used to like the inside of an inn better than the outside yourself. You were always popping in, on duty or off.'

'And so I would be still, Sam, if I could. But don't be hard on me. What can I do? You know how I went for a Shirriff seven years ago, before any of this began. Gave me a chance of walking round the country and seeing folk, and hearing the news, and knowing where the good beer was. But now it's different.'

'But you can give it up, stop Shirriffing, if it has stopped being a respectable job,' said Sam.

'We're not allowed to,' said Robin.

'If I hear *not allowed* much oftener,' said Sam, 'I'm going to get angry.'

'Can't say as I'd be sorry to see it,' said Robin lowering his voice. 'If we all got angry together something might be done. But it's these Men, Sam, the Chief's Men. He sends them round everywhere, and if any of us small folk stand up for our rights, they drag him off to the Lockholes. They took old Flourdumpling, old Will Whitfoot the Mayor, first, and they've taken a lot more. Lately it's been getting worse. Often they beat 'em now.'

'Then why do you do their work for them?' said Sam angrily. 'Who sent you to Frogmorton?'

'No one did. We stay here in the big Shirriff-house. We're the First Eastfarthing Troop now. There's hundreds of Shirriffs all told, and they want more, with all these new rules. Most of them are in it against their will, but not all. Even in the Shire there are some as like minding other folk's business and talking big. And there's worse than that: there's a few as do spy-work for the Chief and his Men.'

'Ah! So that's how you had news of us, is it?'

'That's right. We aren't allowed to send by it now, but they use the old Quick Post service, and keep special runners at different points. One came in from Whitfurrows last night with a "secret message", and another took it on from here. And a message came back this afternoon saying you was to be arrested and taken to Bywater, not direct to the Lockholes. The Chief wants to see you at once, evidently.'

'He won't be so eager when Mr. Frodo has finished with him,' said Sam.

The Shirriff-house at Frogmorton was as bad as the Bridge-house. It had only one storey, but it had the same narrow windows, and it was built of ugly pale bricks, badly laid. Inside it was damp and cheerless, and supper was served on a long bare table that had not been scrubbed for weeks. The food deserved no better setting. The travellers were glad to leave the place. It was about eighteen miles to Bywater, and they set off at ten o'clock in the morning. They would have started earlier, only the delay so plainly annoyed the Shirriff-leader. The west wind had shifted northward and it was turning colder, but the rain was gone.

It was rather a comic cavalcade that left the village, though the few folk that came out to stare at the 'get-up' of the travellers did not seem quite sure whether laughing was allowed. A dozen Shirriffs had been told off as escort to the 'prisoners'; but Merry made them march in front, while Frodo and his friends rode behind. Merry, Pippin, and Sam sat at their ease laughing and talking and singing, while the Shirriffs stumped along trying to look stern and important. Frodo, however, was silent and looked rather sad and thoughtful.

The last person they passed was a sturdy old gaffer clipping a hedge. 'Hullo, hullo!' he jeered. 'Now who's arrested who?'

Two of the Shirriffs immediately left the party and went towards him. 'Leader!' said Merry. 'Order your fellows back to their places at once, if you don't want me to deal with them!'

The two hobbits at a sharp word from the leader came back sulkily. 'Now get on!' said Merry, and after that the travellers saw to it that their ponies' pace was quick enough to push the Shirriffs along as fast as they could go. The sun came out, and in spite of the chilly wind they were soon puffing and sweating.

At the Three-Farthing Stone they gave it up. They had done nearly fourteen miles with only one rest at noon. It was now three o'clock. They were hungry and very footsore and they could not stand the pace.

'Well, come along in your own time!' said Merry. 'We are going on.'

'Good-bye, Cock-robin!' said Sam. 'I'll wait for you outside *The Green Dragon*, if you haven't forgotten where that is. Don't dawdle on the way!'

'You're breaking arrest, that's what you're doing,' said the leader ruefully, 'and I can't be answerable.'

'We shall break a good many things yet, and not ask you to answer,' said Pippin. 'Good luck to you!'

The travellers trotted on, and as the sun began to sink towards the White Downs far away on the western horizon they came to Bywater by its wide pool; and there they had their first really painful shock. This was Frodo and Sam's own country, and they found out now that they cared about it more than any other place in the world. Many of the houses that they had known were missing. Some seemed to have been burned down. The pleasant row of old hobbit-holes in the bank on the north side of the Pool were deserted, and their little gardens that used to run down bright to the water's edge were rank with weeds. Worse, there was a whole line of the ugly new houses all along Pool Side, where the Hobbiton Road ran close to the bank. An avenue of trees had stood there. They were all gone. And looking with dismay up the road towards Bag End they saw a tall chimney of brick in the distance. It was pouring out black smoke into the evening air.

Sam was beside himself. 'I'm going right on, Mr. Frodo!' he cried. 'I'm going to see what's up. I want to find my gaffer.'

'We ought to find out first what we're in for, Sam,' said Merry. 'I guess that the "Chief" will have a gang of ruffians handy. We had better find someone who will tell us how things are round here.'

But in the village of Bywater all the houses and holes were shut, and no one greeted them. They wondered at this, but they soon discovered the reason of it. When they reached *The Green Dragon*, the last house on the Hobbiton side, now lifeless and with broken windows, they were disturbed to see half a dozen large ill-favoured Men lounging against the inn-wall; they were squint-eyed and sallow-faced.

'Like that friend of Bill Ferny's at Bree,' said Sam.

'Like many that I saw at Isengard,' muttered Merry.

The ruffians had clubs in their hands and horns by their belts, but they had no other weapons, as far as could be seen. As the travellers rode up they left the wall and walked into the road, blocking the way.

'Where d'you think you're going?' said one, the largest and most evil-looking of the crew. 'There's no road for you any further. And where are those precious Shirriffs?'

'Coming along nicely,' said Merry. 'A little footsore, perhaps. We promised to wait for them here.'

'Garn, what did I say?' said the ruffian to his mates. 'I told Sharkey it was no good trusting those little fools. Some of our chaps ought to have been sent.'

'And what difference would that have made, pray?' said Merry. 'We are not used to footpads in this country, but we know how to deal with them.'

'Footpads, eh?' said the man. 'So that's your tone, is it? Change it, or we'll change it for you. You little folk are getting too uppish. Don't you trust too much in the Boss's kind heart. Sharkey's come now, and he'll do what Sharkey says.'

'And what may that be?' said Frodo quietly.

'This country wants waking up and setting to rights,' said the ruffian, 'and Sharkey's going to do it; and make it hard, if you drive him to it. You need a bigger Boss. And you'll get one before the year is out, if there's any more trouble. Then you'll learn a thing or two, you little rat-folk.'

'Indeed. I am glad to hear of your plans,' said Frodo. 'I am on my way to call on Mr. Lotho, and he may be interested to hear of them too.'

The ruffian laughed. 'Lotho! He knows all right. Don't you worry. He'll do what Sharkey says. Because if a Boss gives trouble, we can change him. See? And if little folks try to push in where they're not wanted, we can put them out of mischief. See?'

'Yes, I see,' said Frodo. 'For one thing, I see that you're behind the times and the news here. Much has happened since you left the South. Your day is over, and all other ruffians'. The Dark Tower has fallen, and there is a King in Gondor. And Isengard has been destroyed, and your precious master is a beggar in the wilderness. I passed him on the road. The King's messengers will ride up the Greenway now, not bullies from Isengard.'

The man stared at him and smiled. 'A beggar in the wilderness!' he mocked. 'Oh, is he indeed? Swagger it, swagger it, my little cock-a-whoop. But that won't stop us living in this

fat little country where you have lazed long enough. And' –
he snapped his fingers in Frodo's face – 'King's messengers!
That for them! When I see one, I'll take notice, perhaps.'

This was too much for Pippin. His thoughts went back to
the Field of Cormallen, and here was a squint-eyed rascal
calling the Ring-bearer 'little cock-a-whoop'. He cast back
his cloak, flashed out his sword, and the silver and sable of
Gondor gleamed on him as he rode forward.

'I am a messenger of the King,' he said. 'You are speaking
to the King's friend, and one of the most renowned in all the
lands of the West. You are a ruffian and a fool. Down on
your knees in the road and ask pardon, or I will set this troll's
bane in you!'

The sword glinted in the westering sun. Merry and Sam
drew their swords also and rode up to support Pippin; but
Frodo did not move. The ruffians gave back. Scaring Bree-
land peasants, and bullying bewildered hobbits, had been
their work. Fearless hobbits with bright swords and grim
faces were a great surprise. And there was a note in the voices
of these newcomers that they had not heard before. It chilled
them with fear.

'Go!' said Merry. 'If you trouble this village again, you will
regret it.' The three hobbits came on, and then the ruffians
turned and fled, running away up the Hobbiton Road; but
they blew their horns as they ran.

'Well, we've come back none too soon,' said Merry.

'Not a day too soon. Perhaps too late, at any rate to save
Lotho,' said Frodo. 'Miserable fool, but I am sorry for him.'

'Save Lotho? Whatever do you mean?' said Pippin.
'Destroy him, I should say.'

'I don't think you quite understand things, Pippin,' said
Frodo. 'Lotho never meant things to come to this pass. He
has been a wicked fool, but he's caught now. The ruffians
are on top, gathering, robbing and bullying, and running or
ruining things as they like, in his name. And not in his name
even for much longer. He's a prisoner in Bag End now, I
expect, and very frightened. We ought to try and rescue him.'

'Well I am staggered!' said Pippin. 'Of all the ends to our journey that is the very last I should have thought of: to have to fight half-orcs and ruffians in the Shire itself – to rescue Lotho Pimple!'

'Fight?' said Frodo. 'Well, I suppose it may come to that. But remember: there is to be no slaying of hobbits, not even if they have gone over to the other side. Really gone over, I mean; not just obeying ruffians' orders because they are frightened. No hobbit has ever killed another on purpose in the Shire, and it is not to begin now. And nobody is to be killed at all, if it can be helped. Keep your tempers and hold your hands to the last possible moment!'

'But if there are many of these ruffians,' said Merry, 'it will certainly mean fighting. You won't rescue Lotho, or the Shire, just by being shocked and sad, my dear Frodo.'

'No,' said Pippin. 'It won't be so easy scaring them a second time. They were taken by surprise. You heard that horn-blowing? Evidently there are other ruffians near at hand. They'll be much bolder when there's more of them together. We ought to think of taking cover somewhere for the night. After all we're only four, even if we are armed.'

'I've an idea,' said Sam. 'Let's go to old Tom Cotton's down South Lane! He always was a stout fellow. And he has a lot of lads that were all friends of mine.'

'No!' said Merry. 'It's no good "getting under cover". That is just what people have been doing, and just what these ruffians like. They will simply come down on us in force, corner us, and then drive us out, or burn us in. No, we have got to do something at once.'

'Do what?' said Pippin.

'Raise the Shire!' said Merry. 'Now! Wake all our people! They hate all this, you can see: all of them except perhaps one or two rascals, and a few fools that want to be important, but don't at all understand what is really going on. But Shire-folk have been so comfortable so long they don't know what to do. They just want a match, though, and they'll go up in fire. The Chief's Men must know that. They'll try to stamp on us and put us out quick. We've only got a very short time.

'Sam, you can make a dash for Cotton's farm, if you like. He's the chief person round here, and the sturdiest. Come on! I am going to blow the horn of Rohan, and give them all some music they have never heard before.'

They rode back to the middle of the village. There Sam turned aside and galloped off down the lane that led south to Cotton's. He had not gone far when he heard a sudden clear horn-call go up ringing into the sky. Far over hill and field it echoed; and so compelling was that call that Sam himself almost turned and dashed back. His pony reared and neighed.

'On, lad! On!' he cried. 'We'll be going back soon.'

Then he heard Merry change the note, and up went the Horn-cry of Buckland, shaking the air.

> *Awake! Awake! Fear, Fire, Foes! Awake!*
> *Fire, Foes! Awake!*

Behind him Sam heard a hubbub of voices and a great din and slamming of doors. In front of him lights sprang out in the gloaming; dogs barked; feet came running. Before he got to the lane's end there was Farmer Cotton with three of his lads, Young Tom, Jolly, and Nick, hurrying towards him. They had axes in their hands, and barred the way.

'Nay! It's not one of them ruffians,' Sam heard the farmer say. 'It's a hobbit by the size of it, but all dressed up queer. Hey!' he cried. 'Who are you, and what's all this to-do?'

'It's Sam, Sam Gamgee. I've come back.'

Farmer Cotton came up close and stared at him in the twilight. 'Well!' he exclaimed. 'The voice is right, and your face is no worse than it was, Sam. But I should a' passed you in the street in that gear. You've been in foreign parts, seemingly. We feared you were dead.'

'That I ain't!' said Sam. 'Nor Mr. Frodo. He's here and his friends. And that's the to-do. They're raising the Shire.

We're going to clear out these ruffians, and their Chief too. We're starting now.'

'Good, good!' cried Farmer Cotton. 'So it's begun at last! I've been itching for trouble all this year, but folks wouldn't help. And I've had the wife and Rosie to think of. These ruffians don't stick at nothing. But come on now, lads! Bywater is up! We must be in it!'

'What about Mrs. Cotton and Rosie?' said Sam. 'It isn't safe yet for them to be left all alone.'

'My Nibs is with them. But you can go and help him, if you have a mind,' said Farmer Cotton with a grin. Then he and his sons ran off towards the village.

Sam hurried to the house. By the large round door at the top of the steps from the wide yard stood Mrs. Cotton and Rosie, and Nibs in front of them grasping a hay-fork.

'It's me!' shouted Sam as he trotted up. 'Sam Gamgee! So don't try prodding me, Nibs. Anyway, I've a mail-shirt on me.'

He jumped down from his pony and went up the steps. They stared at him in silence. 'Good evening, Mrs. Cotton!' he said. 'Hullo, Rosie!'

'Hullo, Sam!' said Rosie. 'Where've you been? They said you were dead; but I've been expecting you since the Spring. You haven't hurried, have you?'

'Perhaps not,' said Sam abashed. 'But I'm hurrying now. We're setting about the ruffians, and I've got to get back to Mr. Frodo. But I thought I'd have a look and see how Mrs. Cotton was keeping, and you, Rosie.'

'We're keeping nicely, thank you,' said Mrs. Cotton. 'Or should be, if it weren't for these thieving ruffians.'

'Well, be off with you!' said Rosie. 'If you've been looking after Mr. Frodo all this while, what d'you want to leave him for, as soon as things look dangerous?'

This was too much for Sam. It needed a week's answer, or none. He turned away and mounted his pony. But as he started off, Rosie ran down the steps.

'I think you look fine, Sam,' she said. 'Go on now! But

take care of yourself, and come straight back as soon as you have settled the ruffians!'

When Sam got back he found the whole village roused. Already, apart from many younger lads, more than a hundred sturdy hobbits were assembled with axes, and heavy hammers, and long knives, and stout staves; and a few had hunting-bows. More were still coming in from outlying farms.

Some of the village-folk had lit a large fire, just to enliven things, and also because it was one of the things forbidden by the Chief. It burned bright as night came on. Others at Merry's orders were setting up barriers across the road at each end of the village. When the Shirriffs came up to the lower one they were dumbfounded; but as soon as they saw how things were, most of them took off their feathers and joined in the revolt. The others slunk away.

Sam found Frodo and his friends by the fire talking to old Tom Cotton, while an admiring crowd of Bywater folk stood round and stared.

'Well, what's the next move?' said Farmer Cotton.

'I can't say,' said Frodo, 'until I know more. How many of these ruffians are there?'

'That's hard to tell,' said Cotton. 'They moves about and comes and goes. There's sometimes fifty of them in their sheds up Hobbiton way; but they go out from there roving round, thieving or "gathering" as they call it. Still there's seldom less than a score round the Boss, as they names him. He's at Bag End, or was; but he don't go outside the grounds now. No one's seen him at all, in fact, for a week or two; but the Men don't let no one go near.'

'Hobbiton's not their only place, is it?' said Pippin.

'No, more's the pity,' said Cotton. 'There's a good few down south in Longbottom and by Sarn Ford, I hear; and some more lurking in the Woody End; and they've sheds at Waymeet. And then there's the Lockholes, as they call 'em: the old storage-tunnels at Michel Delving that they've made into prisons for those as stand up to them. Still I reckon there's not above three hundred of them in the Shire all told, and maybe less. We can master them, if we stick together.'

'Have they got any weapons?' asked Merry.

'Whips, knives, and clubs, enough for their dirty work: that's all they've showed so far,' said Cotton. 'But I dare say they've got other gear, if it comes to fighting. Some have bows, anyway. They've shot one or two of our folk.'

'There you are, Frodo!' said Merry. 'I knew we should have to fight. Well, they started the killing.'

'Not exactly,' said Cotton. 'Leastways not the shooting. Tooks started that. You see, your dad, Mr. Peregrin, he's never had no truck with this Lotho, not from the beginning: said that if anyone was going to play the chief at this time of day, it would be the right Thain of the Shire and no upstart. And when Lotho sent his Men they got no change out of him. Tooks are lucky, they've got those deep holes in the Green Hills, the Great Smials and all, and the ruffians can't come at 'em; and they won't let the ruffians come on their land. If they do, Tooks hunt 'em. Tooks shot three for prowling and robbing. After that the ruffians turned nastier. And they keep a pretty close watch on Tookland. No one gets in nor out of it now.'

'Good for the Tooks!' cried Pippin. 'But someone is going to get in again, now. I am off to the Smials. Anyone coming with me to Tuckborough?'

Pippin rode off with half a dozen lads on ponies. 'See you soon!' he cried. 'It's only fourteen miles or so over the fields. I'll bring you back an army of Tooks in the morning.' Merry blew a horn-call after them as they rode off into the gathering night. The people cheered.

'All the same,' said Frodo to all those who stood near, 'I wish for no killing; not even of the ruffians, unless it must be done, to prevent them from hurting hobbits.'

'All right!' said Merry. 'But we shall be having a visit from the Hobbiton gang any time now, I think. They won't come just to talk things over. We'll try to deal with them neatly, but we must be prepared for the worst. Now I've got a plan.'

'Very good,' said Frodo. 'You make the arrangements.'

Just then some hobbits, who had been sent out towards Hobbiton, came running in. 'They're coming!' they said. 'A score or more. But two have gone off west across country.'

'To Waymeet, that'll be,' said Cotton, 'to fetch more of the gang. Well, it's fifteen mile each way. We needn't trouble about them just yet.'

Merry hurried off to give orders. Farmer Cotton cleared the street, sending everyone indoors, except the older hobbits who had weapons of some sort. They had not long to wait. Soon they could hear loud voices, and then the tramping of heavy feet. Presently a whole squad of the ruffians came down the road. They saw the barrier and laughed. They did not imagine that there was anything in this little land that would stand up to twenty of their kind together.

The hobbits opened the barrier and stood aside. 'Thank you!' the Men jeered. 'Now run home to bed before you're whipped.' Then they marched along the street shouting: 'Put those lights out! Get indoors and stay there! Or we'll take fifty of you to the Lockholes for a year. Get in! The Boss is losing his temper.'

No one paid any heed to their orders; but as the ruffians passed, they closed in quietly behind and followed them. When the Men reached the fire there was Farmer Cotton standing all alone warming his hands.

'Who are you, and what d'you think you're doing?' said the ruffian-leader.

Farmer Cotton looked at him slowly. 'I was just going to ask you that,' he said. 'This isn't your country, and you're not wanted.'

'Well, you're wanted anyhow,' said the leader. 'We want you. Take him lads! Lockholes for him, and give him something to keep him quiet!'

The Men took one step forward and stopped short. There rose a roar of voices all round them, and suddenly they were aware that Farmer Cotton was not all alone. They were surrounded. In the dark on the edge of the firelight stood a ring of hobbits that had crept up out of the shadows. There was nearly two hundred of them, all holding some weapon.

Merry stepped forward. 'We have met before,' he said to the leader, 'and I warned you not to come back here. I warn you again: you are standing in the light and you are covered by archers. If you lay a finger on this farmer, or on anyone else, you will be shot at once. Lay down any weapons that you have!'

The leader looked round. He was trapped. But he was not scared, not now with a score of his fellows to back him. He knew too little of hobbits to understand his peril. Foolishly he decided to fight. It would be easy to break out.

'At 'em, lads!' he cried. 'Let 'em have it!'

With a long knife in his left hand and a club in the other he made a rush at the ring, trying to burst out back towards Hobbiton. He aimed a savage blow at Merry who stood in his way. He fell dead with four arrows in him.

That was enough for the others. They gave in. Their weapons were taken from them, and they were roped together, and marched off to an empty hut that they had built themselves, and there they were tied hand and foot, and locked up under guard. The dead leader was dragged off and buried.

'Seems almost too easy after all, don't it?' said Cotton. 'I said we could master them. But we needed a call. You came back in the nick o' time, Mr. Merry.'

'There's more to be done still,' said Merry. 'If you're right in your reckoning, we haven't dealt with a tithe of them yet. But it's dark now. I think the next stroke must wait until morning. Then we must call on the Chief.'

'Why not now?' said Sam. 'It's not much more than six o'clock. And I want to see my gaffer. D'you know what's come of him, Mr. Cotton?'

'He's not too well, and not too bad, Sam,' said the farmer. 'They dug up Bagshot Row, and that was a sad blow to him. He's in one of them new houses that the Chief's Men used to build while they still did any work other than burning and thieving: not above a mile from the end of Bywater. But he comes around to me, when he gets a chance, and I see he's better fed than some of the poor bodies. All against *The Rules*, of course. I'd have had him with me, but that wasn't allowed.'

'Thank'ee indeed, Mr. Cotton, and I'll never forget it,' said Sam. 'But I want to see him. That Boss and that Sharkey, as they spoke of, they might do a mischief up there before the morning.'

'All right, Sam,' said Cotton. 'Choose a lad or two, and go and fetch him to my house. You'll not have need to go near the old Hobbiton village over Water. My Jolly here will show you.'

Sam went off. Merry arranged for look-outs round the village and guards at the barriers during the night. Then he and Frodo went off with Farmer Cotton. They sat with the family in the warm kitchen, and the Cottons asked a few polite questions about their travels, but hardly listened to the answers: they were far more concerned with events in the Shire.

'It all began with Pimple, as we call him,' said Farmer Cotton; 'and it began as soon as you'd gone off, Mr. Frodo. He'd funny ideas, had Pimple. Seems he wanted to own everything himself, and then order other folk about. It soon came out that he already did own a sight more than was good for him; and he was always grabbing more, though where he got the money was a mystery: mills and malt-houses and inns, and farms, and leaf-plantations. He'd already bought Sandyman's mill before he came to Bag End, seemingly.

'Of course he started with a lot of property in the South-farthing which he had from his dad; and it seems he'd been selling a lot o' the best leaf, and sending it away quietly for a year or two. But at the end o' last year he began sending away loads of stuff, not only leaf. Things began to get short, and winter coming on, too. Folk got angry, but he had his answer. A lot of Men, ruffians mostly, came with great wag-gons, some to carry off the goods south-away, and others to stay. And more came. And before we knew where we were they were planted here and there all over the Shire, and were felling trees and digging and building themselves sheds and houses just as they liked. At first goods and damage was paid for by Pimple; but soon they began lording it around and taking what they wanted.

'Then there was a bit of trouble, but not enough. Old Will the Mayor set off for Bag End to protest, but he never got there. Ruffians laid hands on him and took and locked him up in a hole in Michel Delving, and there he is now. And after that, it would be soon after New Year, there wasn't no more Mayor, and Pimple called himself Chief Shirriff, or just Chief, and did as he liked; and if anyone got "uppish" as they called it, they followed Will. So things went from bad to worse. There wasn't no smoke left, save for the Men; and the Chief didn't hold with beer, save for his Men, and closed all the inns; and everything except Rules got shorter and shorter, unless one could hide a bit of one's own when the ruffians went round gathering stuff up "for fair distribution": which meant they got it and we didn't, except for the leavings which you could have at the Shirriff-houses, if you could stomach them. All very bad. But since Sharkey came it's been plain ruination.'

'Who is this Sharkey?' said Merry. 'I heard one of the ruffians speak of him.'

'The biggest ruffian o' the lot, seemingly,' answered Cotton. 'It was about last harvest, end o' September maybe, that we first heard of him. We've never seen him, but he's up at Bag End; and he's the real Chief now, I guess. All the ruffians do what he says; and what he says is mostly: hack, burn, and ruin; and now it's come to killing. There's no longer even any bad sense in it. They cut down trees and let 'em lie, they burn houses and build no more.

'Take Sandyman's mill now. Pimple knocked it down almost as soon as he came to Bag End. Then he brought in a lot o' dirty-looking Men to build a bigger one and fill it full o' wheels and outlandish contraptions. Only that fool Ted was pleased by that, and he works there cleaning wheels for the Men, where his dad was the Miller and his own master. Pimple's idea was to grind more and faster, or so he said. He's got other mills like it. But you've got to have grist before you can grind; and there was no more for the new mill to do than for the old. But since Sharkey came they don't grind no more corn at all. They're always a-hammering and a-letting out a smoke and a stench, and there isn't no peace even at night in Hobbiton. And they pour out filth a purpose; they've fouled all the lower Water, and it's getting down into Brandywine. If they want to make the Shire into a desert, they're going the right way about it. I don't believe that fool of a Pimple's behind all this. It's Sharkey, I say.'

'That's right!' put in Young Tom. 'Why, they even took Pimple's old ma, that Lobelia, and he was fond of her, if no one else was. Some of the Hobbiton folk, they saw it. She comes down the lane with her old umberella. Some of the ruffians were going up with a big cart.

' "Where be you a-going?" says she.

' "To Bag End," says they.

' "What for?" says she.

' "To put up some sheds for Sharkey," says they.

' "Who said you could?" says she.

' "Sharkey," says they. "So get out o' the road, old hagling!"

' "I'll give you Sharkey, you dirty thieving ruffians!" says she, and ups with her umberella and goes for the leader, near twice her size. So they took her. Dragged her off to the Lockholes, at her age too. They've took others we miss more, but there's no denying she showed more spirit than most.'

Into the middle of this talk came Sam, bursting in with his gaffer. Old Gamgee did not look much older, but he was a little deafer.

'Good evening, Mr. Baggins!' he said. 'Glad indeed I am to see you safe back. But I've a bone to pick with you, in a manner o' speaking, if I may make so bold. You didn't never ought to have a' sold Bag End, as I always said. That's what started all the mischief. And while you've been trapessing in foreign parts, chasing Black Men up mountains from what my Sam says, though what for he don't make clear, they've been and dug up Bagshot Row and ruined my taters!'

'I am very sorry, Mr. Gamgee,' said Frodo. 'But now I've come back, I'll do my best to make amends.'

'Well, you can't say fairer than that,' said the gaffer. 'Mr. *Frodo* Baggins is a real gentlehobbit, I always have said, whatever you may think of some others of the name, begging your pardon. And I hope my Sam's behaved hisself and given satisfaction?'

'Perfect satisfaction, Mr. Gamgee,' said Frodo. 'Indeed, if you will believe it, he's now one of the most famous people in all the lands, and they are making songs about his deeds from here to the Sea and beyond the Great River.' Sam blushed, but he looked gratefully at Frodo, for Rosie's eyes were shining and she was smiling at him.

'It takes a lot o' believing,' said the gaffer, 'though I can see he's been mixing in strange company. What's come of his weskit? I don't hold with wearing ironmongery, whether it wears well or no.'

Farmer Cotton's household and all his guests were up early next morning. Nothing had been heard in the night, but more trouble would certainly come before the day was old. 'Seems as if none o' the ruffians were left up at Bag End,' said Cotton; 'but the gang from Waymeet will be along any time now.'

After breakfast a messenger from the Tookland rode in. He was in high spirits. 'The Thain has raised all our country,' he said, 'and the news is going like fire all ways. The ruffians that were watching our land have fled off south, those that escaped alive. The Thain has gone after them, to hold off the big gang down that way; but he's sent Mr. Peregrin back with all the other folk he can spare.'

The next news was less good. Merry, who had been out

all night, came riding in about ten o'clock. 'There's a big band about four miles away,' he said. 'They're coming along the road from Waymeet, but a good many stray ruffians have joined up with them. There must be close on a hundred of them; and they're fire-raising as they come. Curse them!'

'Ah! This lot won't stay to talk, they'll kill, if they can,' said Farmer Cotton. 'If Tooks don't come sooner, we'd best get behind cover and shoot without arguing. There's got to be some fighting before this is settled, Mr. Frodo.'

The Tooks did come sooner. Before long they marched in, a hundred strong, from Tuckborough and the Green Hills with Pippin at their head. Merry now had enough sturdy hobbitry to deal with the ruffians. Scouts reported that they were keeping close together. They knew that the countryside had risen against them, and plainly meant to deal with the rebellion ruthlessly, at its centre in Bywater. But however grim they might be, they seemed to have no leader among them who understood warfare. They came on without any precautions. Merry laid his plans quickly.

The ruffians came tramping along the East Road, and without halting turned up the Bywater Road, which ran for some way sloping up between high banks with low hedges on top. Round a bend, about a furlong from the main road, they met a stout barrier of old farm-carts upturned. That halted them. At the same moment they became aware that the hedges on both sides, just above their heads, were all lined with hobbits. Behind them other hobbits now pushed out some more waggons that had been hidden in a field, and so blocked the way back. A voice spoke to them from above.

'Well, you have walked into a trap,' said Merry. 'Your fellows from Hobbiton did the same, and one is dead and the rest are prisoners. Lay down your weapons! Then go back twenty paces and sit down. Any who try to break out will be shot.'

But the ruffians could not now be cowed so easily. A few of them obeyed, but were immediately set on by their fellows.

A score or more broke back and charged the waggons. Six were shot, but the remainder burst out, killing two hobbits, and then scattering across country in the direction of the Woody End. Two more fell as they ran. Merry blew a loud horn-call, and there were answering calls from a distance.

'They won't get far,' said Pippin. 'All that country is alive with our hunters now.'

Behind, the trapped Men in the lane, still about four score, tried to climb the barrier and the banks, and the hobbits were obliged to shoot many of them or hew them with axes. But many of the strongest and most desperate got out on the west side, and attacked their enemies fiercely, being now more bent on killing than escaping. Several hobbits fell, and the rest were wavering, when Merry and Pippin, who were on the east side, came across and charged the ruffians. Merry himself slew the leader, a great squint-eyed brute like a huge orc. Then he drew his forces off, encircling the last remnant of the Men in a wide ring of archers.

At last all was over. Nearly seventy of the ruffians lay dead on the field, and a dozen were prisoners. Nineteen hobbits were killed, and some thirty were wounded. The dead ruffians were laden on waggons and hauled off to an old sand-pit nearby and there buried: in the Battle Pit, as it was afterwards called. The fallen hobbits were laid together in a grave on the hill-side, where later a great stone was set up with a garden about it. So ended the Battle of Bywater, 1419, the last battle fought in the Shire, and the only battle since the Greenfields, 1147, away up in the Northfarthing. In consequence, though it happily cost very few lives, it has a chapter to itself in the Red Book, and the names of all those who took part were made into a Roll, and learned by heart by Shire-historians. The very considerable rise in the fame and fortune of the Cottons dates from this time; but at the top of the Roll in all accounts stand the names of Captains Meriadoc and Peregrin.

Frodo had been in the battle, but he had not drawn sword,

and his chief part had been to prevent the hobbits in their wrath at their losses, from slaying those of their enemies who threw down their weapons. When the fighting was over, and the later labours were ordered, Merry, Pippin, and Sam joined him, and they rode back with the Cottons. They ate a late midday meal, and then Frodo said with a sigh: 'Well, I suppose it is time now that we dealt with the "Chief".'

'Yes indeed; the sooner the better,' said Merry. 'And don't be too gentle! He's responsible for bringing in these ruffians, and for all the evil they have done.'

Farmer Cotton collected an escort of some two dozen sturdy hobbits. 'For it's only a guess that there is no ruffians left at Bag End,' he said. 'We don't know.' Then they set out on foot. Frodo, Sam, Merry, and Pippin led the way.

It was one of the saddest hours in their lives. The great chimney rose up before them; and as they drew near the old village across the Water, through rows of new mean houses along each side of the road, they saw the new mill in all its frowning and dirty ugliness: a great brick building straddling the stream, which it fouled with a steaming and stinking outflow. All along the Bywater Road every tree had been felled.

As they crossed the bridge and looked up the Hill they gasped. Even Sam's vision in the Mirror had not prepared him for what they saw. The Old Grange on the west side had been knocked down, and its place taken by rows of tarred sheds. All the chestnuts were gone. The banks and hedgerows were broken. Great waggons were standing in disorder in a field beaten bare of grass. Bagshot Row was a yawning sand and gravel quarry. Bag End up beyond could not be seen for a clutter of large huts.

'They've cut it down!' cried Sam. 'They've cut down the Party Tree!' He pointed to where the tree had stood under which Bilbo had made his Farewell Speech. It was lying lopped and dead in the field. As if this was the last straw Sam burst into tears.

A laugh put an end to them. There was a surly hobbit

lounging over the low wall of the mill-yard. He was grimy-faced and black-handed. 'Don't 'ee like it, Sam?' he sneered. 'But you always was soft. I thought you'd gone off in one o' them ships you used to prattle about, sailing, sailing. What d'you want to come back for? We've work to do in the Shire now.'

'So I see,' said Sam. 'No time for washing, but time for wall-propping. But see here, Master Sandyman, I've a score to pay in this village, and don't you make it any longer with your jeering, or you'll foot a bill too big for your purse.'

Ted Sandyman spat over the wall. 'Garn!' he said. 'You can't touch me. I'm a friend o' the Boss's. But he'll touch you all right, if I have any more of your mouth.'

'Don't waste any more words on the fool, Sam!' said Frodo. 'I hope there are not many more hobbits that have become like this. It would be a worse trouble than all the damage the Men have done.'

'You are dirty and insolent, Sandyman,' said Merry. 'And also very much out of your reckoning. We are just going up the Hill to remove your precious Boss. We have dealt with his Men.'

Ted gaped, for at that moment he first caught sight of the escort that at a sign from Merry now marched over the bridge. Dashing back into the mill he ran out with a horn and blew it loudly.

'Save your breath!' laughed Merry. 'I've a better.' Then lifting up his silver horn he winded it, and its clear call rang over the Hill; and out of the holes and sheds and shabby houses of Hobbiton the hobbits answered, and came pouring out, and with cheers and loud cries they followed the company up the road to Bag End.

At the top of the lane the party halted, and Frodo and his friends went on; and they came at last to the once beloved place. The garden was full of huts and sheds, some so near the old westward windows that they cut off all their light. There were piles of refuse everywhere. The door was scarred; the bell-chain was dangling loose, and the bell would not ring. Knocking brought no answer. At length they pushed and the door yielded. They went in. The place stank and was full of filth and disorder: it did not appear to have been used for some time.

'Where is that miserable Lotho hiding?' said Merry. They had searched every room and found no living thing save rats and mice. 'Shall we turn on the others to search the sheds?'

'This is worse than Mordor!' said Sam. 'Much worse in a way. It comes home to you, as they say; because it is home, and you remember it before it was all ruined.'

'Yes, this is Mordor,' said Frodo. 'Just one of its works. Saruman was doing its work all the time, even when he thought he was working for himself. And the same with those that Saruman tricked, like Lotho.'

Merry looked round in dismay and disgust. 'Let's get out!' he said. 'If I had known all the mischief he had caused, I should have stuffed my pouch down Saruman's throat.'

'No doubt, no doubt! But you did not, and so I am able to welcome you home.' There standing at the door was Saruman himself, looking well-fed and well-pleased; his eyes gleamed with malice and amusement.

A sudden light broke on Frodo. 'Sharkey!' he cried.

Saruman laughed. 'So you have heard the name, have you? All my people used to call me that in Isengard, I believe. A sign of affection, possibly.* But evidently you did not expect to see me here.'

'I did not,' said Frodo. 'But I might have guessed. A little mischief in a mean way: Gandalf warned me that you were still capable of it.'

'Quite capable,' said Saruman, 'and more than a little. You made me laugh, you hobbit-lordlings, riding along with all those great people, so secure and so pleased with your little selves. You thought you had done very well out of it all, and

---

* It was probably Orkish in origin: *sharkû*, 'old man'.

could now just amble back and have a nice quiet time in the country. Saruman's home could be all wrecked, and he could be turned out, but no one could touch yours. Oh no! Gandalf would look after your affairs.'

Saruman laughed again. 'Not he! When his tools have done their task he drops them. But you must go dangling after him, dawdling and talking, and riding round twice as far as you needed. "Well," thought I, "if they're such fools, I will get ahead of them and teach them a lesson. One ill turn deserves another." It would have been a sharper lesson, if only you had given me a little more time and more Men. Still I have already done much that you will find it hard to mend or undo in your lives. And it will be pleasant to think of that and set it against my injuries.'

'Well, if that is what you find pleasure in,' said Frodo, 'I pity you. It will be a pleasure of memory only, I fear. Go at once and never return!'

The hobbits of the villages had seen Saruman come out of one of the huts, and at once they came crowding up to the door of Bag End. When they heard Frodo's command, they murmured angrily:

'Don't let him go! Kill him! He's a villain and a murderer. Kill him!'

Saruman looked round at their hostile faces and smiled. 'Kill him!' he mocked. 'Kill him, if you think there are enough of you, my brave hobbits!' He drew himself up and stared at them darkly with his black eyes. 'But do not think that when I lost all my goods I lost all my power! Whoever strikes me shall be accursed. And if my blood stains the Shire, it shall wither and never again be healed.'

The hobbits recoiled. But Frodo said: 'Do not believe him! He has lost all power, save his voice that can still daunt you and deceive you, if you let it. But I will not have him slain. It is useless to meet revenge with revenge: it will heal nothing. Go, Saruman, by the speediest way!'

'Worm! Worm!' Saruman called; and out of a nearby hut came Wormtongue, crawling, almost like a dog. 'To the road

again, Worm!' said Saruman. 'These fine fellows and lord-
lings are turning us adrift again. Come along!'

Saruman turned to go, and Wormtongue shuffled after
him. But even as Saruman passed close to Frodo a knife
flashed in his hand, and he stabbed swiftly. The blade turned
on the hidden mail-coat and snapped. A dozen hobbits, led
by Sam, leaped forward with a cry and flung the villain to
the ground. Sam drew his sword.

'No, Sam!' said Frodo. 'Do not kill him even now. For he
has not hurt me. And in any case I do not wish him to be
slain in this evil mood. He was great once, of a noble kind
that we should not dare to raise our hands against. He is
fallen, and his cure is beyond us; but I would still spare him,
in the hope that he may find it.'

Saruman rose to his feet, and stared at Frodo. There was
a strange look in his eyes of mingled wonder and respect and
hatred. 'You have grown, Halfling,' he said. 'Yes, you have
grown very much. You are wise, and cruel. You have robbed
my revenge of sweetness, and now I must go hence in bitterness, in debt to your mercy. I hate it and you! Well, I go and
I will trouble you no more. But do not expect me to wish
you health and long life. You will have neither. But that is
not my doing. I merely foretell.'

He walked away, and the hobbits made a lane for him to
pass; but their knuckles whitened as they gripped on their
weapons. Wormtongue hesitated, and then followed his
master.

'Wormtongue!' called Frodo. 'You need not follow him. I
know of no evil you have done to me. You can have rest and
food here for a while, until you are stronger and can go your
own ways.'

Wormtongue halted and looked back at him, half prepared
to stay. Saruman turned. 'No evil?' he cackled. 'Oh no! Even
when he sneaks out at night it is only to look at the stars.
But did I hear someone ask where poor Lotho is hiding? You
know, don't you, Worm? Will you tell them?'

Wormtongue cowered down and whimpered: 'No, no!'

'Then I will,' said Saruman. 'Worm killed your Chief, poor little fellow, your nice little Boss. Didn't you, Worm? Stabbed him in his sleep, I believe. Buried him, I hope; though Worm has been very hungry lately. No, Worm is not really nice. You had better leave him to me.'

A look of wild hatred came into Wormtongue's red eyes. 'You told me to; you made me do it,' he hissed.

Saruman laughed. 'You do what Sharkey says, always, don't you, Worm? Well, now he says: follow!' He kicked Wormtongue in the face as he grovelled, and turned and made off. But at that something snapped: suddenly Wormtongue rose up, drawing a hidden knife, and then with a snarl like a dog he sprang on Saruman's back, jerked his head back, cut his throat, and with a yell ran off down the lane. Before Frodo could recover or speak a word, three hobbit-bows twanged and Wormtongue fell dead.

To the dismay of those that stood by, about the body of Saruman a grey mist gathered, and rising slowly to a great height like smoke from a fire, as a pale shrouded figure it loomed over the Hill. For a moment it wavered, looking to the West; but out of the West came a cold wind, and it bent away, and with a sigh dissolved into nothing.

Frodo looked down at the body with pity and horror, for as he looked it seemed that long years of death were suddenly revealed in it, and it shrank, and the shrivelled face became rags of skin upon a hideous skull. Lifting up the skirt of the dirty cloak that sprawled beside it, he covered it over, and turned away.

'And that's the end of that,' said Sam. 'A nasty end, and I wish I needn't have seen it; but it's a good riddance.'

'And the very last end of the War, I hope,' said Merry.

'I hope so,' said Frodo and sighed. 'The very last stroke. But to think that it should fall here, at the very door of Bag End! Among all my hopes and fears at least I never expected that.'

'I shan't call it the end, till we've cleared up the mess,' said Sam gloomily. 'And that'll take a lot of time and work.'

CHAPTER IX

THE GREY HAVENS

The clearing up certainly needed a lot of work, but it took less time than Sam had feared. The day after the battle Frodo rode to Michel Delving and released the prisoners from the Lockholes. One of the first that they found was poor Fredegar Bolger, Fatty no longer. He had been taken when the ruffians smoked out a band of rebels that he led from their hidings up in the Brockenbores by the hills of Scary.

'You would have done better to come with us after all, poor old Fredegar!' said Pippin, as they carried him out too weak to walk.

He opened an eye and tried gallantly to smile. 'Who's this young giant with the loud voice?' he whispered. 'Not little Pippin! What's your size in hats now?'

Then there was Lobelia. Poor thing, she looked very old and thin when they rescued her from a dark and narrow cell. She insisted on hobbling out on her own feet; and she had such a welcome, and there was such clapping and cheering when she appeared, leaning on Frodo's arm but still clutching her umbrella, that she was quite touched, and drove away in tears. She had never in her life been popular before. But she was crushed by the news of Lotho's murder, and she would not return to Bag End. She gave it back to Frodo, and went to her own people, the Bracegirdles of Hardbottle.

When the poor creature died next Spring – she was after all more than a hundred years old – Frodo was surprised and much moved: she had left all that remained of her money and of Lotho's for him to use in helping hobbits made homeless by the troubles. So that feud was ended.

Old Will Whitfoot had been in the Lockholes longer than any, and though he had perhaps been treated less harshly than some, he needed a lot of feeding up before he could look the part of Mayor; so Frodo agreed to act as his Deputy, until Mr. Whitfoot was in shape again. The only thing that he did as Deputy Mayor was to reduce the Shirriffs to their proper functions and numbers. The task of hunting out the last remnant of the ruffians was left to Merry and Pippin, and it was soon done. The southern gangs, after hearing the news of the Battle of Bywater, fled out of the land and offered little resistance to the Thain. Before the Year's End the few survivors were rounded up in the woods, and those that surrendered were shown to the borders.

Meanwhile the labour of repair went on apace, and Sam was kept very busy. Hobbits can work like bees when the mood and the need comes on them. Now there were thousands of willing hands of all ages, from the small but nimble ones of the hobbit lads and lasses to the well-worn and horny ones of the gaffers and gammers. Before Yule not a brick was left standing of the new Shirriff-houses or of anything that had been built by 'Sharkey's Men'; but the bricks were used to repair many an old hole, to make it snugger and drier. Great stores of goods and food, and beer, were found that had been hidden away by the ruffians in sheds and barns and deserted holes, and especially in the tunnels at Michel Delving and in the old quarries at Scary; so that there was a great deal better cheer that Yule than anyone had hoped for.

One of the first things done in Hobbiton, before even the removal of the new mill, was the clearing of the Hill and Bag End, and the restoration of Bagshot Row. The front of the new sand-pit was all levelled and made into a large sheltered garden, and new holes were dug in the southward face, back into the Hill, and they were lined with brick. The Gaffer was restored to Number Three; and he said often and did not care who heard it:

'It's an ill wind as blows nobody no good, as I always say. And All's well as ends Better!'

There was some discussion of the name that the new row

should be given. *Battle Gardens* was thought of, or *Better Smials*. But after a while in sensible hobbit-fashion it was just called *New Row*. It was a purely Bywater joke to refer to it as Sharkey's End.

The trees were the worst loss and damage, for at Sharkey's bidding they had been cut down recklessly far and wide over the Shire; and Sam grieved over this more than anything else. For one thing, this hurt would take long to heal, and only his great-grandchildren, he thought, would see the Shire as it ought to be.

Then suddenly one day, for he had been too busy for weeks to give a thought to his adventures, he remembered the gift of Galadriel. He brought the box out and showed it to the other Travellers (for so they were now called by everyone), and asked their advice.

'I wondered when you would think of it,' said Frodo. 'Open it!'

Inside it was filled with a grey dust, soft and fine, in the middle of which was a seed, like a small nut with a silver shale. 'What can I do with this?' said Sam.

'Throw it in the air on a breezy day and let it do its work!' said Pippin.

'On what?' said Sam.

'Choose one spot as a nursery, and see what happens to the plants there,' said Merry.

'But I'm sure the Lady would not like me to keep it all for my own garden, now so many folk have suffered,' said Sam.

'Use all the wits and knowledge you have of your own, Sam,' said Frodo, 'and then use the gift to help your work and better it. And use it sparingly. There is not much here, and I expect every grain has a value.'

So Sam planted saplings in all the places where specially beautiful or beloved trees had been destroyed, and he put a grain of the precious dust in the soil at the root of each. He went up and down the Shire in this labour; but if he paid special attention to Hobbiton and Bywater no one blamed him. And at the end he found that he still had a little of the dust left; so he went to the Three-Farthing Stone, which is as near the centre of the Shire as no matter, and cast it in the air with his blessing. The little silver nut he planted in the Party Field where the tree had once been; and he wondered what would come of it. All through the winter he remained as patient as he could, and tried to restrain himself from going round constantly to see if anything was happening.

Spring surpassed his wildest hopes. His trees began to sprout and grow, as if time was in a hurry and wished to make one year do for twenty. In the Party Field a beautiful young sapling leaped up: it had silver bark and long leaves and burst into golden flowers in April. It was indeed a *mallorn*, and it was the wonder of the neighbourhood. In after years, as it grew in grace and beauty, it was known far and wide and people would come long journeys to see it: the only *mallorn* west of the Mountains and east of the Sea, and one of the finest in the world.

Altogether 1420 in the Shire was a marvellous year. Not only was there wonderful sunshine and delicious rain, in due times and perfect measure, but there seemed something more: an air of richness and growth, and a gleam of a beauty beyond that of mortal summers that flicker and pass upon this Middle-earth. All the children born or begotten in that year, and there were many, were fair to see and strong, and most of them had a rich golden hair that had before been rare among hobbits. The fruit was so plentiful that young hobbits very nearly bathed in strawberries and cream; and later they sat on the lawns under the plum-trees and ate, until they had made piles of stones like small pyramids or the heaped skulls of a conqueror, and then they moved on. And no one was ill, and everyone was pleased, except those who had to mow the grass.

In the Southfarthing the vines were laden, and the yield of 'leaf' was astonishing; and everywhere there was so much

corn that at Harvest every barn was stuffed. The Northfarthing barley was so fine that the beer of 1420 malt was long
remembered and became a byword. Indeed a generation later
one might hear an old gaffer in an inn, after a good pint of
well-earned ale, put down his mug with a sigh: 'Ah! that was
proper fourteen-twenty, that was!'

Sam stayed at first at the Cottons' with Frodo; but when
the New Row was ready he went with the Gaffer. In addition
to all his other labours he was busy directing the cleaning up
and restoring of Bag End; but he was often away in the Shire
on his forestry work. So he was not at home in early March
and did not know that Frodo had been ill. On the thirteenth
of that month Farmer Cotton found Frodo lying on his bed;
he was clutching a white gem that hung on a chain about his
neck and he seemed half in a dream.

'It is gone for ever,' he said, 'and now all is dark and
empty.'

But the fit passed, and when Sam got back on the twenty-
fifth, Frodo had recovered, and he said nothing about himself.
In the meanwhile Bag End had been set in order, and Merry
and Pippin came over from Crickhollow bringing back all
the old furniture and gear, so that the old hole soon looked
very much as it always had done.

When all was at last ready Frodo said: 'When are you
going to move in and join me, Sam?'

Sam looked a bit awkward.

'There is no need to come yet, if you don't want to,' said
Frodo. 'But you know the Gaffer is close at hand, and he
will be very well looked after by Widow Rumble.'

'It's not that, Mr. Frodo,' said Sam, and he went very red.

'Well, what is it?'

'It's Rosie, Rose Cotton,' said Sam. 'It seems she didn't
like my going abroad at all, poor lass; but as I hadn't spoken,
she couldn't say so. And I didn't speak, because I had a job
to do first. But now I have spoken, and she says: "Well,
you've wasted a year, so why wait longer?" "Wasted?" I says.

"I wouldn't call it that." Still I see what she means. I feel torn in two, as you might say.'

'I see,' said Frodo: 'you want to get married, and yet you want to live with me in Bag End too? But my dear Sam, how easy! Get married as soon as you can, and then move in with Rosie. There's room enough in Bag End for as big a family as you could wish for.'

And so it was settled. Sam Gamgee married Rose Cotton in the Spring of 1420 (which was also famous for its weddings), and they came and lived at Bag End. And if Sam thought himself lucky, Frodo knew that he was more lucky himself; for there was not a hobbit in the Shire that was looked after with such care. When the labours of repair had all been planned and set going he took to a quiet life, writing a great deal and going through all his notes. He resigned the office of Deputy Mayor at the Free Fair that mid-summer, and dear old Will Whitfoot had another seven years of presiding at Banquets.

Merry and Pippin lived together for some time at Crickhollow, and there was much coming and going between Buckland and Bag End. The two young Travellers cut a great dash in the Shire with their songs and their tales and their finery, and their wonderful parties. 'Lordly' folk called them, meaning nothing but good; for it warmed all hearts to see them go riding by with their mail-shirts so bright and their shields so splendid, laughing and singing songs of far away; and if they were now large and magnificent, they were unchanged otherwise, unless they were indeed more fairspoken and more jovial and full of merriment than ever before.

Frodo and Sam, however, went back to ordinary attire, except that when there was need they both wore long grey cloaks, finely woven and clasped at the throat with beautiful brooches; and Mr. Frodo wore always a white jewel on a chain that he often would finger.

All things now went well, with hope always of becoming

still better; and Sam was as busy and as full of delight as even a hobbit could wish. Nothing for him marred that whole year, except for some vague anxiety about his master. Frodo dropped quietly out of all the doings of the Shire, and Sam was pained to notice how little honour he had in his own country. Few people knew or wanted to know about his deeds and adventures; their admiration and respect were given mostly to Mr. Meriadoc and Mr. Peregrin and (if Sam had known it) to himself. Also in the autumn there appeared a shadow of old troubles.

One evening Sam came into the study and found his master looking very strange. He was very pale and his eyes seemed to see things far away.

'What's the matter, Mr. Frodo?' said Sam.

'I am wounded,' he answered, 'wounded; it will never really heal.'

But then he got up, and the turn seemed to pass, and he was quite himself the next day. It was not until afterwards that Sam recalled that the date was October the sixth. Two years before on that day it was dark in the dell under Weathertop.

Time went on, and 1421 came in. Frodo was ill again in March, but with a great effort he concealed it, for Sam had other things to think about. The first of Sam and Rosie's children was born on the twenty-fifth of March, a date that Sam noted.

'Well, Mr. Frodo,' he said. 'I'm in a bit of a fix. Rose and me had settled to call him Frodo, with your leave; but it's not *him*, it's *her*. Though as pretty a maidchild as any one could hope for, taking after Rose more than me, luckily. So we don't know what to do.'

'Well, Sam,' said Frodo, 'what's wrong with the old customs? Choose a flower name like Rose. Half the maidchildren in the Shire are called by such names, and what could be better?'

'I suppose you're right, Mr. Frodo,' said Sam. 'I've heard

some beautiful names on my travels, but I suppose they're
a bit too grand for daily wear and tear, as you might say.
The Gaffer, he says: "Make it short, and then you won't
have to cut it short before you can use it." But if it's to be
a flower-name, then I don't trouble about the length: it must
be a beautiful flower, because, you see, I think she is very
beautiful, and is going to be beautifuller still.'

Frodo thought for a moment. 'Well, Sam, what about
elanor, the sun-star, you remember the little golden flower in
the grass of Lothlórien?'

'You're right again, Mr. Frodo!' said Sam delighted.
'That's what I wanted.'

Little Elanor was nearly six months old, and 1421 had
passed to its autumn, when Frodo called Sam into the
study.

'It will be Bilbo's Birthday on Thursday, Sam,' he said.
'And he will pass the Old Took. He will be a hundred and
thirty-one!'

'So he will!' said Sam. 'He's a marvel!'

'Well, Sam,' said Frodo, 'I want you to see Rose and find
out if she can spare you, so that you and I can go off together.
You can't go far or for a long time now, of course,' he said
a little wistfully.

'Well, not very well, Mr. Frodo.'

'Of course not. But never mind. You can see me on my
way. Tell Rose that you won't be away very long, not more
than a fortnight; and you'll come back quite safe.'

'I wish I could go all the way with you to Rivendell, Mr.
Frodo, and see Mr. Bilbo,' said Sam. 'And yet the only place
I really want to be in is here. I am that torn in two.'

'Poor Sam! It will feel like that, I am afraid,' said Frodo.
'But you will be healed. You were meant to be solid and
whole, and you will be.'

In the next day or two Frodo went through his papers and
his writings with Sam, and he handed over his keys. There

was a big book with plain red leather covers; its tall pages were now almost filled. At the beginning there were many leaves covered with Bilbo's thin wandering hand; but most of it was written in Frodo's firm flowing script. It was divided into chapters but Chapter 80 was unfinished, and after that were some blank leaves. The title page had many titles on it, crossed out one after another, so:

My Diary. My Unexpected Journey. There and Back Again. And What Happened After.

Adventures of Five Hobbits. The Tale of the Great Ring, compiled by Bilbo Baggins from his own observations and the accounts of his friends. What we did in the War of the Ring.

Here Bilbo's hand ended and Frodo had written:

THE DOWNFALL
OF THE
LORD OF THE RINGS
AND THE
RETURN OF THE KING

(as seen by the Little People; being the memoirs of Bilbo and Frodo of the Shire, supplemented by the accounts of their friends and the learning of the Wise.)

Together with extracts from Books of Lore translated by Bilbo in Rivendell.

'Why, you have nearly finished it, Mr. Frodo!' Sam exclaimed. 'Well, you have kept at it, I must say.'

'I have quite finished, Sam,' said Frodo. 'The last pages are for you.'

On September the twenty-first they set out together, Frodo on the pony that had borne him all the way from Minas Tirith, and was now called Strider; and Sam on his beloved

Bill. It was a fair golden morning, and Sam did not ask where they were going: he thought he could guess.

They took the Stock Road over the hills and went towards the Woody End, and they let their ponies walk at their leisure. They camped in the Green Hills, and on September the twenty-second they rode gently down into the beginning of the trees as afternoon was wearing away.

'If that isn't the very tree you hid behind when the Black Rider first showed up, Mr. Frodo!' said Sam pointing to the left. 'It seems like a dream now.'

It was evening, and the stars were glimmering in the eastern sky as they passed the ruined oak and turned and went on down the hill between the hazel-thickets. Sam was silent, deep in his memories. Presently he became aware that Frodo was singing softly to himself, singing the old walking-song, but the words were not quite the same.

> *Still round the corner there may wait*
> *A new road or a secret gate;*
> *And though I oft have passed them by,*
> *A day will come at last when I*
> *Shall take the hidden paths that run*
> *West of the Moon, East of the Sun.*

And as if in answer, from down below, coming up the road out of the valley, voices sang:

> *A! Elbereth Gilthoniel!*
> *silivren penna miriel*
> *o menel aglar elenath,*
> *Gilthoniel, A! Elbereth!*
> *We still remember, we who dwell*
> *In this far land beneath the trees*
> *The starlight on the Western Seas.*

Frodo and Sam halted and sat silent in the soft shadows, until they saw a shimmer as the travellers came towards them.

There was Gildor and many fair Elven folk; and there to Sam's wonder rode Elrond and Galadriel. Elrond wore a mantle of grey and had a star upon his forehead, and a silver harp was in his hand, and upon his finger was a ring of gold with a great blue stone, Vilya, mightiest of the Three. But Galadriel sat upon a white palfrey and was robed all in glimmering white, like clouds about the Moon; for she herself seemed to shine with a soft light. On her finger was Nenya, the ring wrought of *mithril*, that bore a single white stone flickering like a frosty star. Riding slowly behind on a small grey pony, and seeming to nod in his sleep, was Bilbo himself.

Elrond greeted them gravely and graciously, and Galadriel smiled upon them. 'Well, Master Samwise,' she said. 'I hear and see that you have used my gift well. The Shire shall now be more than ever blessed and beloved.' Sam bowed, but found nothing to say. He had forgotten how beautiful the Lady was.

Then Bilbo woke up and opened his eyes. 'Hullo, Frodo!' he said. 'Well, I have passed the Old Took today! So that's settled. And now I think I am quite ready to go on another journey. Are you coming?'

'Yes, I am coming,' said Frodo. 'The Ring-bearers should go together.'

'Where are you going, Master?' cried Sam, though at last he understood what was happening.

'To the Havens, Sam,' said Frodo.

'And I can't come.'

'No, Sam. Not yet anyway, not further than the Havens. Though you too were a Ring-bearer, if only for a little while. Your time may come. Do not be too sad, Sam. You cannot be always torn in two. You will have to be one and whole, for many years. You have so much to enjoy and to be, and to do.'

'But,' said Sam, and tears started in his eyes, 'I thought

you were going to enjoy the Shire, too, for years and years, after all you have done.'

'So I thought too, once. But I have been too deeply hurt, Sam. I tried to save the Shire, and it has been saved, but not for me. It must often be so, Sam, when things are in danger: some one has to give them up, lose them, so that others may keep them. But you are my heir: all that I had and might have had I leave to you. And also you have Rose, and Elanor; and Frodo-lad will come, and Rosie-lass, and Merry, and Goldilocks, and Pippin; and perhaps more that I cannot see. Your hands and your wits will be needed everywhere. You will be the Mayor, of course, as long as you want to be, and the most famous gardener in history; and you will read things out of the Red Book, and keep alive the memory of the age that is gone, so that people will remember the Great Danger and so love their beloved land all the more. And that will keep you as busy and as happy as anyone can be, as long as your part of the Story goes on.

'Come now, ride with me!'

Then Elrond and Galadriel rode on; for the Third Age was over, and the Days of the Rings were passed, and an end was come of the story and song of those times. With them went many Elves of the High Kindred who would no longer stay in Middle-earth; and among them, filled with a sadness that was yet blessed and without bitterness, rode Sam, and Frodo, and Bilbo, and the Elves delighted to honour them.

Though they rode through the midst of the Shire all the evening and all the night, none saw them pass, save the wild creatures; or here and there some wanderer in the dark who saw a swift shimmer under the trees, or a light and shadow flowing through the grass as the Moon went westward. And when they had passed from the Shire, going about the south skirts of the White Downs, they came to the Far Downs, and to the Towers, and looked on the distant Sea; and so they rode down at last to Mithlond, to the Grey Havens in the long firth of Lune.

As they came to the gates Círdan the Shipwright came forth to greet them. Very tall he was, and his beard was long, and he was grey and old, save that his eyes were keen as stars; and he looked at them and bowed, and said: 'All is now ready.'

Then Círdan led them to the Havens, and there was a white ship lying, and upon the quay beside a great grey horse stood a figure robed all in white awaiting them. As he turned and came towards them Frodo saw that Gandalf now wore openly on his hand the Third Ring, Narya the Great, and the stone upon it was red as fire. Then those who were to go were glad, for they knew that Gandalf also would take ship with them.

But Sam was now sorrowful at heart, and it seemed to him that if the parting would be bitter, more grievous still would be the long road home alone. But even as they stood there, and the Elves were going aboard, and all was being made ready to depart, up rode Merry and Pippin in great haste. And amid his tears Pippin laughed.

'You tried to give us the slip once before and failed, Frodo,' he said. 'This time you have nearly succeeded, but you have failed again. It was not Sam, though, that gave you away this time, but Gandalf himself!'

'Yes,' said Gandalf; 'for it will be better to ride back three together than one alone. Well, here at last, dear friends, on the shores of the Sea comes the end of our fellowship in Middle-earth. Go in peace! I will not say: do not weep; for not all tears are an evil.'

Then Frodo kissed Merry and Pippin, and last of all Sam, and went aboard; and the sails were drawn up, and the wind blew, and slowly the ship slipped away down the long grey firth; and the light of the glass of Galadriel that Frodo bore glimmered and was lost. And the ship went out into the High Sea and passed on into the West, until at last on a night of rain Frodo smelled a sweet fragrance on the air and heard the sound of singing that came over the water. And then it seemed to him that as in his dream in the house of Bombadil, the grey rain-curtain turned all to silver glass and was rolled back, and he beheld white shores and beyond them a far green country under a swift sunrise.

But to Sam the evening deepened to darkness as he stood at the Haven; and as he looked at the grey sea he saw only a shadow on the waters that was soon lost in the West. There still he stood far into the night, hearing only the sigh and murmur of the waves on the shores of Middle-earth, and the sound of them sank deep into his heart. Beside him stood Merry and Pippin, and they were silent.

At last the three companions turned away, and never again looking back they rode slowly homewards; and they spoke no word to one another until they came back to the Shire, but each had great comfort in his friends on the long grey road.

At last they rode over the downs and took the East Road, and then Merry and Pippin rode on to Buckland; and already they were singing again as they went. But Sam turned to Bywater, and so came back up the Hill, as day was ending once more. And he went on, and there was yellow light, and fire within; and the evening meal was ready, and he was expected. And Rose drew him in, and set him in his chair, and put little Elanor upon his lap.

He drew a deep breath. 'Well, I'm back,' he said.